Ben

TIMOTHY J. HANRATTY

Ben

ARPress
ILLUMINATING IDEAS
EMPOWERING VOICES

ARPress
45 Dan Road Suite 36
Canton MA 02021

Hotline: 1(800) 220-7660
Fax: 1(855) 752-6001

Ordering Information:
Quantity Sales. Special discounts are available on quantity purchases by corporations, associations, and others. For details, contact the publisher at the address above.

Printed in the United States of America.

ISBN-13   Paperback   979-8-89389-624-4
            eBook   979-8-89389-625-1

Library of Congress Control Number: 2024921505

CHAPTER 1

He could run and hop like a rabbit or a fox in the grass. It would appear that he was darting and dancing as prey evading a predator. On the contrary, he was doing the chasing of a far more nimble and familiar foe. It was the small, grey, furry Creature, the squirrel. It was his number 1 nemesis as he always grew close, but never could catch the creature before it jumped on to a tree and climbed away to safety, where he could not follow. He heard her voice, the pack leader and his master calling his name in the distance. It was at that moment his second most hated antagonist dropped from the tree and flew by his nose before landing in the green wet grass still not warmed by the big, yellow circle above. (The Sun) He began to give chase of the feathery creature when she called out his name again, louder and impatiently, "BEN!" His legs were moving and he yelped as she watched him in his bed. He opened his eyes and lifted his head following the sound of her calling his name, "BEN.....BEN She was waiting with his leash for him to come. He opened his eyes and jumped to his feet as he usually did and responded by her side dutifully. She attached him to the leash, and he was happy to follow where ever she might lead. In his mind he was wishfully thinking it was where he was when his eyes were closed. They passed the place where he was many times before. It was the place that he stood by waiting for her patiently. He did not know what a window was, but he had stood by it many days waiting for her. He knew instinctually when she would return. The big yellow, warm circle (Sun) was cooling down when she was close. He knew that. He also knew that it was a place that he visited when his eyes were closed. He knew nothing of memory, but he was there when his eyes were opened and when they were closed. They went off in the thing, the car, that led to the place of his happiness when his eyes were closed and open. It was Ramapo State Park. He chased his enemies around and followed her diligently. He relieved himself and she spoke lovingly to him. It was there time alone together.

When they returned home to their pack he ate his food and watched the little people eat theirs. The big person that she loved was there also and the entire pack was together. The big yellow circle was gone for the day. He was growing tired as was the entire pack. When she went up to her bed he followed. It was not his own bed, but he liked it more being next to her as did the big person that she loved. He shared his affection with her dutifully. He knew she loved the little people most and then the big person. He was happy to be loved by her in his order of the pack. He closed his eyes next to her and was soon in another place. It was not the green grass chasing his enemies. He was being chased himself by the ones like him from the pack nearby. They were trying to catch him and were nipping at his tail. Sometimes he played with them and other times they attacked him. He ran and ran. His legs were moving, and he was barking. He did not know what dreams were. Then he felt her touch him and speak to him lovingly as he opened his eyes. He gazed at her and felt love and closed his eyes drifting back to sleep happily.

Time carried on and the little people grew to be big people as he found it harder and painful to pursue his enemies. Time moves continuously as all living things follow the cycle and process of life within the constant, inexplicable concept of TIME. The little people were now big people. They were once preborn people. It was impossible for Ben to distinguish the difference of his experiences of happiness when his eyes closed from when they were open. In another context, preborn fully developed people have experiences within the resting mind. There is no frame of reference or developed experience that allows for understanding the difference of conscious and unconscious thought. The mind is vastly complex and mysterious. The sensation of 'déjà vu' is the mis- filing of an experience from short term memory to long term memory and then it corrects itself. It is complex and mysterious. Many of life's great and wonderful mysteries can be accepted by faith with the resolve that the mind can not solve all mysteries.

CHAPTER 2

Ben knew nothing of thought processes as he waited by the window for her and watched for her to return. He was dreaming and knew nothing else. He knew the feeling of Love and to wait for her. She would be back soon. He knew by the warmth and light of the yellow circle above. (the Sun) He felt her move and get up so he opened his eyes and watched her, waiting to determine what he was to do next. His dreaming of waiting for her was the same as his reality. There was no differentiation in his mind. He felt the same emotions.

The exceptional bond and emotion of love transcends the comprehension of difference between conscious and unconscious thought. It did not matter if he was seeing her with his eyes opened or closed. Likewise, the in-utero fetus, fully developed human knows not of memory and has no experiences other than the safety and warmth of the fluid filled world in the womb. The dreams of a preborn human are not recalled. The bond and emotional love of the mother and child is certain. The new human does not recall the pre born experience, but the attachment and bond are proven by the mother's instinct to nurture. It is proven by the instincts of the newborn to take to the mothers nutrition supply. The newborn human will take to suckling and attaching to the mother instinctually. Other species of mammals instinctually nurture their newborn young. Many inexplicable, natural processes of life are simply accepted. Dreams are likewise accepted and seldom explored. If Ben had the capacity to reason and comprehend his dreams, he may have recalled his siblings of his first pack and the days he suckled his birth mother. The mysteries of the mind, for example, dreaming, existence and other unexplained phenomena are a highway traveling through barriers such as dimensions and TIME. Quite possibly between life and after life. The minds power to see alternate dimensions of experiences in dreams is closer than any scientific explanation. The unconscious state of mind and dreaming of life is quite possibly the highway of greater understanding. As Ben, the K-9, can not reason and solve mathematical formulas, the human can not solve the mystery of life and then the after life. The mind feels happiness at times and the body feels health simultaneously. When the mind is sad the body weeps in the form of illness. There is a balance of peace in mind and body.

Ben felt anxious when she called to him to come. He knew the tone of her voice. The tremble, the slightest emotion. He could sense her tone instinctually. At times you wake up with your heart racing and in fear that what you were experiencing unconsciously was real. In a few moments you realize that it was all a dream. In time the dream will fade from the mind. What seemed very real is completely cleared from any memory. Such is the mystery of the mind. But the sound of her voice was a memory he had when his eyes were opened and closed. He knew she called him to come to go to a place that was not the grass with his enemies to chase. The times they he followed her through the day and chased after the enemies and she was happy. This was a different trip they had made times before to the place with strange big people. He was placed on a table, touched, and pricked painfully as she watched and felt very upset. He did not like seeing her that way. He knew that is where they were going. That was the place in his bad unconscious mind. The mind has thoughts that are buried deep and sometimes they resurface. The mind at times can not retrieve a memory such as a dream when it is sought for and then at times a thought resurfaces triggered unknowingly. Thus is the mysterious complexity of the mind.

He was lying on the table in the room looking at her. She stroked his head and side and his eyes closed. He drifted into the unconscious world rather than look at her in sadness. She watched his legs moving and heard his yelping. He was off and running through the field of green. She wept as she waited for the veterinarian to return. She anticipated that it was time for a final prick of a needle that would render him unconscious forever. It would be convenient and simple to think all that he had for knowledge was instinct and learned behavior. He could not account for his memory and emotions. How could he comprehend otherwise? He opened his eyes when the doctor entered the room again. He focused on her and experienced her sadness as she talked to the doctor. He wanted to jump up and into her arms but knew better so he sat obediently and awaited. His name was Ben. He, was a Maltese, Yorkshire terrier mix. Often called a morkie. A cute, small dog that is loyal, obedient, and rather of high intellect in the canine species. Dogs of his mixed breed became notable in the fable of 'Benji' and the film, 'Wizard of Oz' as ToTo. She named him Ben and often lovably called him gentle Ben. He was gritty, territorial and protective over her (his master). The affectionate term gentle Ben reminded her of the leg of a skiing slope. It was a memory that resided in her dreams. When she was younger she went skiing with her love, Alex. It was long before she met John and been married. She and Alex would spend long weekends at the catamount resort skiing and having fun. The gentle Ben branch was a break off of the advanced slope 500 meters from the mountain top. It was marked as moderate, but it felt far from its marked designation. She had her own dreams of those warm memories from long ago. Lately, her dreams were of sadness or she did not recall them. Her dreams in the parallel dimension with Alex were seldom. The visits to her parallel dimension in her dreams, where she would sit by the fire and then make love with Alex after a fun day on the slopes were less frequent. It may have been repressed. Painful unconscious thoughts can be suppressed naturally to save the body pain, as the human body always heals itself. Alex had died a tragic death and it wounded her deeply, perhaps permanently. Parallel dimensions are different existences that occur in time and are incapable of being processed by the mind. The unconscious mind and traumatized mind can see and comprehend as it has no barrier to the highway that surpasses the three-dimensional sense. It is not time travel. There is no explanation of TIME, Existence is the closest explanation. The nearest explanation of time is only proved by the unconscious mind traveling on the highway from one dimension to another. Her conscious mind was currently being traumatized with thought of losing her little dog and best friend, Ben. That was the reason she had her mind opened and the highway to another dimension led her to Alex. She wept as Ben looked on at her. Ben was helpless as he sat and waited for her command. If only he could do something to please her. He knew nothing of her pain as she wept for Alex and HIM knowing he may be put down and go to the place that his eyes closed forever.

Her minds natural defense took her down the highway to another place in time. She was sitting by a warm fireplace drinking wine and eating cheese and thin herb flavored water crackers. They would soon begin to kiss and then make love. The adventure to another dimension was abruptly concluded when the doctor came back into the room. Donna had no conscious thought of her transcendental experience until the Veterinarian, Dr Belmont, began to speak. Then it struck her as an electrical shock through the body, from head to toe as if she had grabbed an electrical outlet without the protection from its receptacle case. Ben stared at her expressions changing. She was there in the room with Ben on the table. Dr. Belmont began to speak, "Donna,", and he cleared his throat, "Mrs. Murphy, I would like to review the results of the tests with you." The gravity of his tone momentarily forced her mind to slip to a thought of wanting to be someplace else. Her stomach felt a tinge of tightening inside. She had to focus on his words. Her mind flashed to a time when she was young and had been told she had an ingrown hair on her head. It was long ago. She had a procedure that surgically removed the problem, but not before the damage was done, as the blood vessels in her brain were compromised by the infiltration. She grew and lived a healthy life and mostly forgot the traumatic events. The flash to the past was over and she listened intensely. Ben stared at her focusing on her eyes that grew intense. He was pleased to see her in the same state she would be when scolding the little people. She was no longer crying so he began wagging his tail. Dr. Belmont went on, "the results show that his tumors have reduced in size and his blood tests are normal." Then he continued, "the only explanation I can offer is that your Love for him and the medicine provided a miracle. He is healthy and you can take him home." She began to weep involuntarily, this time, tears of joy. Ben could sense the difference and nearly jumped into her arms, but she thrust herself forward and grabbed him first. She called him off the table. His tail wagged fast as he extended his head to lick her face as she connected his leash to his collar. As she leads him out to the car, he grabbed the leash in his mouth and jerked it signaling to her. She knew he wanted to play and most likely go to the park to walk beside her and then chase off his adversaries. They had not gone there in a while. He was relieved that she was smiling and happy again. She was emotionally exhausted and only wanted to go home with him to tell the good news to the family and take a nap, They returned home and she explained as best she could that Ben was going to be alright and that she needed to go lie down. She curled up in bed and he nuzzled next to her. Before she faded to unconscious, she thought of the flash back to her surgery she underwent when she was fourteen. It was traumatizing, but she recovered. Could the sensitivity of her brain have been affected? Why did she travel to another place in time, to a different dimension? Was it real? She drifted off to unconscious holding Ben warmly, happy that he was safe. She thought for certain he was going to die. If not today, then when? Further, when would she die? The absolute mystery of life and death had not unsettled her until today. The time travel through to a dimension of the past was coincided by the flashback to her brain trauma. Then she was off to a restful sleep.

CHAPTER 3

A sound awakened her, and her eyes opened slowly. The sound was not an alarm clock or loud sudden door slamming. It was a faint, distant cry, like that of one of her children crying. As she opened her eyes, she felt the soft movement next to her. It was Ben. She watched him moving his legs and heard him whimper. He was dreaming as she had witnessed many times before. She knew what he was dreaming of and she shook him to wake him up. He popped up quickly and licked her face. She decided to take him to the place in his dreams. After all, he had a long day so far. After telling John and the children, they were off to the park. They walked side by side and she let him off the leash. He chased after the squirrels and birds and then came back to her. It was mid afternoon, and the sun was approaching the tree line, but there were no shadows yet. They continued the path around the park. She often dreamed on their walks. The thoughts of the morning moved through her mind. She wondered about the way she transcended to another place in time. That and what could have saved Ben. This mystery reminded her of a story she read or had been told. She could not be certain. The Roman Emperor and philosopher, Marcus Aurelius, was walking on the beach and pondering the mystery of the trilogy. The Christian belief of the Father, the son, and the holy spirit when an ANGEL was sent to him in the form of a boy. The boy appeared on the beach and asked, what he was thinking and when Marcus Aurelius explained the mystery he was deeply laboring over the boy dug a hole in the sand and took a bucket to the sea. He filled the bucket with ocean water and filled the hole in the sand with it and he continued to do so as he looked to the emperor and said "I will continue to do this and drain the water from the ocean into this hole before you solve your mystery." Donna smiled as she walked and watched Ben running and playing happy and healthy. What could have saved him? Was it her Love and a miracle? No Angel appeared to her to explain. What happened to her mind that enabled her to transcend time and dimensions? Was it possible for anyone to do? She wanted to rid her mind of the mystery that had been cast upon her. These thoughts would persist and haunt her. She noticed the shadows and the cool breeze of evening. It was time for them to go home for supper. Ben was bouncing with joy and that was good enough for her for the now. He knew by the fading sun that it was time to go too.

She took Ben home and they ate with the pack as usual. It was the end of a long day. It was only the beginning for Donna on the quest to solve the mystery that would haunt her. She began to wonder who she was. The walks with Ben became more than exercise for her and fun for him. He was happy as a puppy again and she lamented over the thoughts. She could never associate him with her dilemma. It must have been coincidental that his health had arisen the questions in her mind. Her husband, John noticed a distant look in her eyes at times and persisted to know what she was thinking, what was eating away at her. Then, on a perfectly sun filled afternoon they were walking near the tree line and as she was distant in her mind , transcended to another place and another time , he pulled free and was off chasing his hated enemy, the grey, furry creature. She had gazed off to the river beside the tree line and the sounds and sights had taken her to a place in time when she walked in the creek with her childhood friend Jenny and looked for little fairies that lived in the banks of the creek under the brush that hung over the bank. The fairies would only come out when it was safe. She knew you could only see them when you feel it and they wanted you to. It was a great feeling. She saw them when she was in that place in time. She wanted to go back to that feeling. She was a child then. She was an adult now and was shocked again back to the present in moments when Ben was off and the tension on her hand where the leash was becoming weightless. She looked up sharply and he was chasing a squirrel up a great, old sycamore tree.

She looked down at the leash that was no longer in her hand. She had dropped it and the reality of the present came back to her. The leash was pulled away with Ben as he ran to pursue his enemies.. She gazed at her empty hand and for some reason focused on the palm of her hand. She instinctually came very close to a defense mechanism taking over and suppressing her mind to abstain from the place it should not go to. It felt too stimulating to resist so she stared more closely at her empty palm.

CHAPTER 4

Donna stared at the lines of her palm and her mind transcended to a different place in time. She was sitting with her cousin, Mary Alice and Mary Alice was teaching her all that she learned about palm reading. The young ladies were both of Christian faith and it was not accepted to believe in heretic ways. Donna's mind was filled with questions from her recent experiences as a woman. She was back with Mary and listening. Mary was explaining that she looked at the palm of her friend Blake's hand and noticed that his lifeline suddenly stopped. She warned Blake about driving too fast as he was a high adrenalin type of young man. He did listen to Mary's concern. She never told him or any one about the life line on his palm until she told Donna as she wept. It was merely two weeks following her warning to Blake that he was driving with two of his friends in his Delorean sports car at a high rate of speed that he could not negotiate a curve in the road and the accident occurred. His two friends survived, but the steering wheel impaled Blake and he died tragically, very young. Mary went on to tell Donna of a tale her uncle told her. Her uncle was an investigator of crime and was attending an autopsy of a suspicious death. The pathologist's assistant remarked that it was no surprise as she observed the young corpse. The lifeline on the hand of the dead was very short. Mary believed in the practice of palm reading and her tales impacted Donna. As Donna stood staring at her own palm she wondered about her life. Could she have read Alex's palm and prevented his tragic death? Should she read her husband John's and her children? Her minds instinct of suppression took over and she looked up to find Ben. He was growing tired of the chasing and inability to capture adversaries. He loped back to her picked up the leash that was dragging beside him. He held it in his jaws and gazed up at her. He was ready to go home. She put her thoughts in a box and closed it for now. Ben would continue to have his dreams. Donna tried not to dwell on her thoughts, but it was impossible.

Ben continued to dream and she would watch him kicking his legs and yelping as he was off to distant place in his mind. She tried to ignore the questions in her conscious mind, but when they went for walks the mysteries continued to haunt her. She would walk and look at the majesty of nature all around her. It seemed that everything triggered her curious mind. For example, the skin from a cicada that remained on a tree trunk. The cicada insect has many species. Approximately every 10-15 years a specific species of Cicada will emerge from the earth in which they burrow to mate and carry on the species. What determines the order and rhythm?

The river always flows gently by leading to the sea. The fairies that live there will not reveal themselves to her. That part of life has passed. Could she go back? Why did the specific Cicada chattering in the warm sun choose this year to emerge? Why did the river continually flow? The thoughts in her mind were moving as a land slide of rock or avalanche of snow. It grew stronger and the pressure grew strong inside her head. As the velocity of the the slide grows in strength so did the pain in her mind. She tried to talk to her husband John about the problem she was having and he attributed the thoughts to stress. She could not explain her thoughts to anyone. Ben was healthy and her family was happy so she decided to keep her thoughts to herself hoping it would pass.

CHAPTER 5

The path was irreversible and back down memory lane she would go. The slightest unknown circumstance could trigger a thought. On another occasion in the park Ben ran off and a man who was walking through the park had befriended him. When Donna saw the man playing with Ben she felt it necessary to retrieve him so off she went across the field of grass. She appeared to be nervously apologetic due to her little animal's behavior, although she knew the man was enjoying his lovable qualities. It was a similar play as watching her toddler children fulfilling the past experiences of elderly women playing with her little ones as they once did with their own children. The look of love and emotion in their eyes was that of a window to all that she was feeling. The past, present and future could be viewed. It was the look of all she felt inside. She could not identify the value of the moment. She was living in the present dimension of time. She apologized for Ben and called his name. He came to her side. The man said the name was Tom and he offered his hand. She took it and told him she was Donna Murphy this was her little Ben Murphy. The adorable, energetic, friendly terrier mix. He was a combination of Benji and Toto. Tom had kind eyes and a soft, warm, friendly handshake. She felt no threat, nor ill will. She rather liked the man. He gave the avuncular feeling to her. She was beginning to spin on her heel to go when Tom said "wait", so she hesitated. He asked if she would let him walk with Ben for a little while to give her time to walk alone. He said, "you look as though you want to walk and think on your own." Identifying her independence. She declined and said, "Ben, you stay by my side", as she pointed, and he followed. She had exhibited who was in command and then said to Tom, "you are welcome to join us," and Tom obeyed as well. He walked on the other side of Ben keeping a respectful distance. She felt a tinge uneasy, having a man other than John being in her company, but he was naturally friendly and so avuncular in his mannerism. Ben was very at ease and she trusted his primordial instinct. They walked and talked about Ben and simple matters. Tom was married for 36 years and had two grown children. She talked vaguely about her husband and two children. Ben ran off to chase a chipmunk that ventured out from the sparse trees. Donna was staring at the old, weathered headstones in the rear of the historical chapel that was adjacent to the park. The inscriptions on the headstones were no longer legible. She had a distant look in her eyes. Tom noticed and asked," are you feeling alright?" She rarely opened her private thoughts to anyone, but she was so overwhelmed with all the thoughts in her mind, she answered his question with one of her own, knowing it was not a polite practice. "Have you ever thought of the dead?" It was her only way she could summon inside of herself to answer what she deemed a personal question.

He knew something was disturbing her. He had noticed her in the park on other occasions and watched her staring into a million miles away. He replied, "yes, loved ones that die will come back to you one day." She thought he could see right through her and felt naked. What was his intention she wondered? She asked him to explain what he meant. Tom then explained that when he was a boy his grandfather passed away and his grandmother explained to him that one day the loved one will visit you again. Donna smiled and said she agreed with him. She felt very at ease talking to him and continued with her thoughts. She revealed all that she had been thinking of, time, dreams, and dimensions. They walked as Ben found his way back to her side. Ben was unusually colliding with her leg between her and this person that was not a pack member. She understood the signal and it hastened her to continue in thought. She had already stated too much and recognized it.

CHAPTER 6

She stopped and told Ben to be polite and sit. Then she asked a second question. "Do you think I am insane?" Tom said, "No, I do not. I think I may be of service to you." Her thoughts of him intensified. She would not allow herself to ask any further questions. She remembered that you learn more by listening than talking so she waited and walked on gesturing with her hand for Ben to follow. It was a signal for Tom to follow as well and he followed the leader. The path through the park led out of the wooded area adjacent to the river and a fork in the path led up a hill. That was the direction that she chose. It looked ominous, like a path to the unknown. Half of the way from the summit she stopped and looked to her right. There was a cavern that was dark. It was a mining hole that had been searched long ago. Donna stared at it and waited for a reaction. Ben stood by her side and waited for her next move. Tom looked at her gazing into the dark hole and finally broke the long silence. He said, "I am a Psychiatrist, ok, I'm not a spy. You look like you need help." She breathed a sigh of relief and felt victorious. He had broken the ice. She wondered, 'should I trust this man and say any thing further, or is it time to walk away?' She broke her gaze away from the dark cavern and turned to meet his eyes. Looking into his eyes, she recognized him. It was the face of the past. This was not a dream. It was a transcending moment to a different place and time. She could see the face of a person that no longer existed. She could see it. The feeling shook her. It was not faith, or believing in something. It was a real experience. This was her proof. She wanted to tell Tom what she was thinking, but contained her thoughts. She gestured for Ben with a wave of her arm and spun on her heel to walk back as she said, "goodbye, I forgot that I have much to do." She walked back down the hill with Ben happily by her side. She heard the faint call of "goodbye for now. "Donna felt a sensation of elation and nervousness all at the same time. She felt her thoughts had been confirmed and she was not insane, yet she knew not the meaning of the occurrences. She walked beside the river and looked for the fairies that live in the banks under the brush. She recognized that was her youthful imagination. The experience outside of the abandoned, old mine was entirely different. This was the cause of her ambivalent feelings. What had she discovered? Was this normal? The questions of existence and time were traveling so wildly at rapid speed in her mind that it was painful. She had to stop thinking and knew it. If she continued to think and discovered the secrets she would die. She ran off into the grass as Ben chased her. She fell to the ground and wrestled around with Ben until she began to cry. Then she sat and looked at the sky as he licked her salt tears from her face. The sun had moved over the trees and shadows now chilled the air. She went home with Ben and said nothing to her family of her thoughts. John and the kids had to be protected from her knowledge. It was her responsibility.

That night she thought deeply about seeing the face of a dead man she knew long ago in a man she hardly knew. Was this a gift or could anyone see what she had? The man she saw was named Uncle Ellison. He was s kind man that lived near her when she was young, and she would visit him. He was a retired draftsman with a gifted hand for drawing. He sketched pictures of animals for her and gave her candy. He was old and kind. He died naturally of old age many years ago. Something about Tom, the psychiatrist brought him back to her. It scared her, seeing his face again. The mine, uncle Elisons face, the fairies, Alex, her Love from the past. It was overwhelming. She crawled into bed and Ben inched closer to her in his spot. John fell into their bed and asked if she was feeling ok. She said she was just tired and told him she loved him. As she lay thinking Ben began kicking his legs as he was off in his dreams.

CHAPTER 7

She thought of Ben dreaming about the park and it was then she knew what she had to do. Being certain she was not insane, she had to test herself. She did not want tell her family nor a psychiatrist of her feelings. She had said enough to Tom the psychiatrist and a stranger and it only produced more confusion. Her thoughts of time, transcendence and dimensions had to be her problem to solve so she thought of a plan as she watched her Ben moving through time in his dream, kicking and yelping. She touched him and he settled down. Her time would come. The following day she took Ben to the park and let him run free to play as she settled on an old blanket by the river edge with some snacks for Ben and lunch for her. She thought it was a crazy idea, but her explanation to anyone of what she was thinking would be equally crazy so this was equally or less crazy and she could do it alone. It would hopefully give her peace in her mind. She sat by the river, listening to the trickling water and awaiting the presence of the fairies to emerge as she scanned the banks of the river and the overgrowth of plants. Her thoughts were telling her this was a crazy idea, but she told herself it was only as crazy as someone having a picnic by themselves as their dog played in the park. If it were a test, it was a test you could not study or prepare for. So maybe it was some form of transcendental IQ test.

Donna unzipped her cooler bag and took out a sandwich and her favorite soft drink. Ben was charging toward her having heard the bag opening as a voice called out, "Mrs. Murphy, is that you, having lunch all alone?" Donna recognized the voice of Tom, the psychiatrist, and she felt annoyed that he was intruding. She really wanted to have a bite of her sandwich, but did not unwrap it. Tom was approaching and Ben was charging still, now even harder to get between her and the man, to protect her. She was the leader of his pack and he would defend her. She turned her head and said, "oh, hi Tom, would you like a sandwich? I only have one Sprite but made two sandwiches. He asked," what did you make? she replied,"Roast beef with cheddar and horseradish Mayo on a roll, my favorite." He said, "sounds great, but I don't eat meat, thanks anyway." She thought that figures. She was happy and did not want his company. He continued, "I thought we could talk." She politely replied, no Thank you." Shutting the door on him. Then Ben slid and slammed into her side. He sat next to her and stared down the stranger. Tom said sorry for intruding and walked off. She said thank you and have a nice day.

She felt a deep relief and thought,'I really didn't want to talk to the shrink', as she unwrapped her sandwich. It looked perfect. A generous ½ inch of red, soft roast beef and thick slices of aged, yellow cheddar cheese with horseradish mayonnaise on a fresh Kaiser roll. She felt her carnivorous urge to sink her teeth into it, but rewarded Ben with a scrap of beef that she peeled off from overhanging the roll. He was rewarded for being her knight and guardian. She had food for him too, but he loved to share with the pack. Donna enjoyed her sandwich with a bag of potato chips and her bottle of sprite. As she finished, she looked around for a garbage Can to throw away the wrapper, bag and napkin. She fed Ben his food by hand and shared some of the meat from her abundantly filled sandwich. He reached his head up to lick her face and she chuckled as she wiped off his affection. She pointed to the river and said drink to him, allowing him to climb down the bank and drink the clear, clean, flowing water. He hesitated when a soft, high pitched voice called out, "no, don't send him here!!!" Donna heard the voice and looked around. She saw no one. She began to rise to go and throw away her trash when the voice called out again, "where are you going Donna? We have been waiting for you for such a longtime." She looked around trying to locate the origin of the voice. The voice continued, "I'm right here, look we live right here, think back." She followed the sound of the voice to the riverbank and then the electrical shock blasted through her from her brain to her toes again. At first sight it was a hummingbird floating above the brush that flowed over the riverbank. As she focused closely her sense of vision was delightfully pleased by the array of colors and eyes. The vision of flight was poetry in motion, and she knew then it was the fairy she knew when she was a girl. Their eyes locked and Donna felt overwhelmed with emotion as she asked in a trembling voice, "is that you?" The reply from the harpsicle voice sounded heavenly, "it is me, retreat, we were waiting for you. You need us now. At that instant, the sun beam coned through an opening in the clouds and shined on them. Donna felt the warmth of the rays and the love of being in her presence. Donna felt an equilibrium flowing through her and could not speak as she stared at all she had been seeking. Lost for words, her mouth agape she tried to gather the strength to speak. Ben was staring at her and waiting. He heard her speaking to someone and his instinct communicated information to him. He had to break her free from her stunned state of consciousness, so he jumped up to her and nudged her with his nose smelling and licking her. Donna broke free from her focused, confused state. Her state of mind felt good. It was warm and tingling her internally. She broke free and placed her hand on his head," good boy." Then she focused on the existence of the being before her and said, "Retreat, I remember you and wish to Thank you for coming back to me. I came here in search of help."

The voice of the fairy , sang out," we are always here to help you. We have TIME as you will understand. We will help you understand in time, be patient. Donna felt at ease and thanked Retreat again and then said, " I will be patient , simply , help me to understand." She felt safe and comforted as two additional fairies appeared, floating up from their hiding place in the bank and floating heavenly in air next to Retreat. They were different yet equally beautiful colors. Retreat melodically spoke," you do remember Galaxy and Sky do you not?" Donna said, "it has been a very long time, but yes I do. I will not let Ben come down and disturb your homes." She hugged Ben and assured him all was ok, she was talking to friends. His tail wagged as he licked her face. "I will go around and get him water down stream.

CHAPTER 8

Donna took her sprite bottle and emptied out any remaining soft drink in the grass and then walked a short ways up stream and stepped down carefully into the bank to the waters edge. She filled the bottle with cool water and climbed back up to pour the water into the cup of her hand as Ben licked it out. The sect leader of the fairy trio, Retreat, was floating in air by her side. She sang out," perhaps it is best if I begin." Donna was pleased and agreed, "yes, please Retreat, help me. Tell me why I am here." Retreat replied,"that is an excellent question and the answer shall reveal itself, but it is best to start from the beginning of your quest, and with you furry friend." The dialogue now begun as Donna said"His name is Ben." Retreat said," I beg your pardon, Ben is the beginning of your journey to this infinite place in time. He is the cause of this effect. So let us start there and you will begin to see." Donna said "I did not see, I thought I was losing him and my mind took me to a different place in time." Retreat said , " Ah, yes , your mind's ability found the way." Donna said, "I guess so, what does it mean?" Retreat,"What place in time? I know it wasn't the first time. You came back to us after your surgery and we visited until you were ready to go back again." Donna asked , "go back where?"

Retreat continued, " I will explain for a time and then galaxy and sky will explain further. The first time you came to us was following your brain surgery you were scared and confused. You felt comfort in coming back to us. This time you were afraid to lose

Ben . Your mind took you away to a safer place before you came back to us, your most cherished safety place. You used your mind to travel here and now you are trying to understand. ". Donna felt the urge to enter into the dialogue and she added, " yes,! Found myself back with my first love, Alex, who died long ago and it startled me." Retreat questioned, " why? It must be the reason you are scared." Donna continued, " I was back in a place that is important to me and it confused me. Alex and I met in school and I became pregnant with a child inside me following a long, fun ski trip weekend. He died in a tragic car accident and I was not certain what to do about the child because I was in school still so I had the pregnancy terminated and continued on with life, but I never could forget the baby girl that I named Shelby. I never knew her , yet I love her and feel as though I do know her.

Retreat interjected, " ok Donna, the first thing you need to understand is that our existence is not one of zero sum. You are intelligent and will see that we do not add and or take away in our existence. You are religious and understand the mystery of faith. I am explaining to you the mystery of existence. There is no zero sum and there is only one constant. The only constant is TIME , which continually moves and we are in it. Existence continually happens and everything is happening all in TIME. I will simplify, Ben is with you right now. Your family was with you today and will be again soon. The past, present and future are all occurring in time. All at the same time. It is the only constant. You Have the ability to see your daughter Shelby. Please ask a question if you Have one,". Donna tried to understand and asked, " why Can I not see Shelby or Alex and talk to them?" Retreat continued, " you haven't touched me , yet you are talking to me." Donna replied, " some would say I am insane. Maybe I should go home now. Donna hesitated, "Wait, I have a question. I have seen pre life and post life humans. Is what I am experiencing a form of mind control? I have no other way to form my question. Can you teach me? Ok, I beg your pardon, that is a multitude of questions. Retreat assured her, " it is ok Donna, all of your questions will be answered. I have begun to explain to you existence. Go home and rest and we will continue on your quest for answers at a different place in time. Go and rest, remember, there is one constant, TIME. TIME and existence continue as we move through them and it's dimensions. They move continuously and simultaneously, that is is the cause. The effect is the different dimensions. Give it time Donna, you have a lot to think about We are always here for you. Donna said goodbye and waved for Ben to follow her to the car to go home. As she began to spin on her heel to turn and walk away she stopped and looked back. She saw the vision of two colors floating and then disappearing into the river bank. She continued to make her way as she bent and rubbed Ben's head and said , " do you see all of the trouble you have started. He enjoyed the attention and emotion as they briskly walked back across the green field to the car. On the way home she thought of making dinner for John and the kids. Then, could she ever explain all of this to them and would they understand? No she decided, not burden them with her thoughts . She told herself to let it go for now and think of what she had at home that she could use to make a good meal. Donna was always very intelligent. She studied biochemistry and business sales of and utilized both as a very successful pharmaceutical sales executive for the worlds largest pharmaceutical drug creator and distributor. She could make her own schedule. Donna had a strong hold on the largest, most profitable accounts due to her effectiveness in the understanding of the chemistry and her ability to persuade in sales. She had always been accomplished and successful at problem solving. At present she was perplexed, but believed in the mystery of faith and was prepared to be patient and learn more. The only constant was TIME. She understood and believed in her new knowledge. The concepts and no zero sum outcome. All existence occurring simultaneously. Yet, the analytical, scientific curious nature of her mind needed more.

CHAPTER 9

S he got home and set up Ben's bowls of water and food. She checked on the kids doing their homework and then emulsified a pesto sauce and set the chicken breast they had in a ziplock bag with the pesto to marinade. It was a pesto chicken sandwich dinner this evening. Then she logged into her lap top and replied to work emails and scheduled meetings. John came home and kissed her head as she focused on the screen of the lap top at the island. He asked if all was ok . Saying she felt distant lately. She told him that the scare with Ben and her upcoming sales conference had been on her mind, consciously not mentioning the major dilemma in her mind, but she was getting better and they had a nice walk in the park that afternoon. It was not her intent to burden her family with the dilemma in her mind. She said she was making grilled chicken pesto sandwiches with jambalaya wild rice for dinner, which he and the kids loved. They exchanged I Love you words and all was good. Ben sat and watched her work. Her mind strayed here and there. It was Wednesday and she had an important client meeting on Friday so the only day she could return to the river would be tomorrow. She tried to tell herself not to pursue the matter any further, but it was impossible to stop thinking about. She felt drawn as a moth is to the light. What fate awaited her, she knew not. That night Donna slept peacefully. Some days she would wake and recall her dreams. If she had a nightmare or bad experience while sleeping she could recall it vaguely for a couple of hours and then it disappeared forever unless she wrote it down. If she did write down the events of a dream or nightmare the notes did not coherently reflect later what she had felt. This morning the thought of her dreams reminded her that this journey of her mind all began with her watching Ben dream. The dreams she had now awakened from this morning were pleasantly vague and equally odd. In her dream she was with her fairy friends , but she was making the presentation to them in a meeting room. It was a combination of her passion for her profession and a back and forth dialogue with her fairy friends. The reflection of her dream paralleled what was in her mind. It was harmless and made logical sense. Ben was next to her, warm and still sleeping. Donna began to stir and wake while John was up and getting ready to head out to work. He was a Sheriff. He regularly dressed and then sat on the bed before leaving to kiss her and tell her he loved her. It was a pre wake up alarm. Donna had nothing on her schedule this morning so she could wake up slow. John touched her and said he would start a pot of coffee for them and then was off to go on duty. She dozed and then was awake thinking. The dream made perfect sense. It raised questions for her. Was she really with her fairy friends? Are the bad dreams/nightmares an alternate, punishing form of reality or a sign of something? She nudged Ben to get him going. It amused her. If she was awake so should he be. He did not want to get up and only curled closer to her making it evident he was happy and clearly not ready to get up just yet. She found it amusing to nudge him more. Donna could smell coffee brewing and could hear the kids stirring around getting up and ready for school. It was time to get moving around in the world. She stretched and began to get up. Ben reluctantly, but obediently followed. They went down to the kitchen. Donna fixed herself a cup of coffee and refreshed Bens bowls with food and water. She called up to the kids as they were getting ready to go. She wrapped pesto chicken sandwiches the night before that they could take to school for lunch, but they declined being that they ate that for dinner the night before. She gave them money to buy lunch at school and that pretty much determined what her lunch would be if she did not get the urge for something different. She logged into her lap top and tried to convince herself that her day was free and open to changes, never consciously thinking that she would go seeking the friends at the river again , but subconsciously it was calling her. Before reviewing her accounts she made herself a light breakfast consisting of scrambled eggs on toast with half of a pink grapefruit. She thought of eating more , because she intended to have the energy to run in the park today. Planning for a run helped to take her mind away from what it was itching at her to do. First things first, another distraction, review her business accounts. She had the largest, most profitable accounts in sales at her corporation. All of her client contracts renewed and paid as if on auto pilot and her salary and bonus commissions reflected handsomely. She made it her practice to communicate and meet with her clients regularly without being aggressive or needy, simply friendly and professional. That was her reputation as well as being intelligent, reliable and efficient. A scan of her accounts, emails and schedule appeared consistent with all of the pieces on the chess board in her favor so she closed the lap top and went about getting dressed for the day. She decided on grey stretch pants and a light Turquoise top over a sports bra with her grey over black ASICS running shoes. The stretch pants revealed her athletically toned legs and above average calf muscles. She packed one of the pesto chicken sandwiches after adding a healthy slice of Havarti dill cheese to it, a bag of potato chips and a bottle of Sprite. She also packed some treats for Ben if he was so deserved and they were off and out to the Jeep.

CHAPTER 10

As Donna drove in the direction of Ramapo state park for her run with Ben she was thinking of other things she could do to avoid the inevitable reason she was going to the park. She was nearing a sandwich and soup shop that she liked very much and wondered what specials they may have prepared for Thursday. The soups were always prepared fresh daily and were complimented by a fresh roll and a piece of fruit of your choice. It was usually an orange or a banana which were equally as fresh as the soup and rolls. She imagined a steeping hot potato leek soup as fresh as in Ireland minus the pint of black Guinness. She shook the thought of Big Al's soup shop and knew she packed lunch as Ben nudged the back of her arm observing that she was drifting away in thought. He knew they were going to the park and helped her refocus. She knew what the nudge implied and focused on the run around the Ramapo park. The State park was a gift of nature. There was a circular loop around a vast field of grass that had a river running beside the west side of the loop. A trail branched off the loop on the west side and ascended to a bird sanctuary where some peered through binoculars in search of eagles, hawks and other birds that nested in the tall trees. Near the top of the rise to the sanctuary were the abandoned mines that bore deep into the hill side. The spot where she turned away from Tom, the psychiatrist who she hoped to not have an unfortunate occasion to see again. He was nice and polite, but far too intrusive and tried to enter her personal zone and it was uncomfortable. Her husband John and the kids were the only ones that were permitted to enter. The dilemma that currently filled her mind was different , she allowed no one in, for now. Donna had an aggressive scientific problem solving mind. This was a problem for her to face and solve on her own. Her nature was to strive, succeed and problem solve which was partly the reason for her earning highest Honors, magna cum in scientific studies and then her reaching the pinnacle of her field in pharmaceutical sales. She was. Innately intelligent as well.

As she turned and entered through the gates of the park Ben grew anxious. He stood up on the seat wagging his tail peering around as if his head was on a swivel. As she drove into the parking area Ben sounded a low growl from his chest. He had observed the man Tom before she did. She saw him and heard the low growl and it made sense. She reached over and stroked his head telling him all was OK. Then she found a parking space that was far enough away. They got out of the car and Donna began to stretch. She let Ben run around the parking area. Tom had been standing by his car she presumed and now he was approaching her. He said, "It is so nice to see you again. Are you ok?" She felt uneasy and somewhat angry and replied,"Hi, I'm fine , we are here for a run so if you don't mind." She continued to stretch hoping he could take the hint. He attempted to play with Ben to prolong his saying goodbye and she knew it. Ben did too so he continued to lead down toward the park. Tom started, "I thought I saw you yesterday by the river. It looked like you were talking to yourself, are you sure everything is ok? We Can talk."

He was polite and kind, but she had enough and stated what came into her mind, " I'm not certain of your intention, and I do not mean to offend, but I would really like to be alone. If I was talking to anyone , it was my Ben." He knew he wasn't welcome so he said his apology for intruding and walked away. To Donna it was a relief. She wanted and needed a good run. It would feel like opening a pressure relief valve.

CHAPTER 11

Donna stretched a little more and then called Ben to go run on the trail loop around the field of grass. He was leashed and was familiar with this activity. He was not to run off in the field. He would run by her side. They were then off running on the gravel path at a mild pace. There were some walkers for exercise and some with dogs. Ben knew it was not time to play with those like him. He had to keep up with his pack leader. They made the half way point on the loop and she felt great in her stride. She always felt good running and really needed this to release the pressure from her mind. The physical exertion took her away from her thoughts until they approached the West leg of the loop that paralleled the river. The loop was formed like a track and field oval, only longer. She found herself gazing at the river looking for her floating friends near the river bank. She could see the water flowing over the rocks and fallen tree branches, but no other sign of activity. The path was some distance away so she was not surprised that nothing could be seen. Ben knew she was off and drifting so he pulled on the leash to bring her back , which was ironic because that is what she normally did to him when he was distracted. She smiled and focused on running strong in stride back to the car. When they reached the parking lot she released Ben from the leash and she walked around and stretched. She went to the car and retrieved a large bottle of Evian water to drink and pour into her palm for Ben to drink. She also gave him a treat of dog bacon which he loved. He enjoyed this bond and time with her. She took the lunch bag cooler out of the Jeep and she looked around. No sign of Tom the shrink she thought, Thank goodness. Then she told Ben to come and they headed back in the direction of the river. He was free to run and chase his adversaries as they crossed the field. She was thinking of a good spot to set down and eat by the river. She had also grabbed the old, cotton southwestern frontier print blanket that she kept in the Jeep . She chose a flat soft grassy area near the river and spread out the blanket and set the lunch bag on it to hold it down. Ben loved sharing food with the pack when they let him and he was eager to do so, but it would have to wait for now. He neared the river bank and peered over the edge. Was he looking for way a down to the water or looking for those his master was talking to, she did not know. Donna called out to him" NO and STOP!!"

A slightly, different yet equally melodious, harp like voice sang out, "thank you Donna." She scanned the River bank for the source of the voice. At first there was nothing, then she could see the colorful floating vision that she recognized from the past. It was long ago, but she knew that it was Galaxy. The fairy spoke, "sky and I are here today to visit with you Donna. Retreat told us that you have many questions and need our help. Please join us in the water and we will walk for a little while.". Donna knew the fairies and remembered walking with them in a river long ago when she was a young girl She moved to sit on the bank and took her running shoes off and socks. She tucked the socks in the shoes and tossed them over to the blanket. She told Ben it was ok and touched him with tug on his head behind the ear to follow her as she walked into the freezing cold river water. It was good for her feet after running she thought. Ben entered and showed no signs of reaction to the cold. Donna stood and braced herself with the shocking chill moving through her blood. The two fairies floated by her side. Galaxy asked her of her thoughts.Donna said, " Retreat helped me understand. We are in it. We are always moving in time. The past, present and future. It is always happening and it is all occurring in different dimensions But my mind works scientifically and I am seeking more proof of existence in TIME and it's relativity. " Donna meant no offense or disrespect, but her stubbornly persistent scientific mind was in search of answers.

Galaxy did not hesitate, "It is certain that Retreat told you, it is so simple." Let us walk and talk." Donna took two steps as Ben sloshed along in the water and the fairies floated by her side.Galaxy started, "did you feel anything when you stepped into the river?" Donna, "I feel the soft sandy mud and stones under my feet and the cold water on my skin" Then Galaxy continued with the examination/sensation of the water temperature." You do not need a thermometer to know the temperature has changed, similarly you will not need a scientific explanation of the warmth of the sun when it is drying-and evaporating the water on your skin." Galaxy told her, " you do not need a slide under a microscope to see or to understand evaporation. Galaxy furthered, that the sun in the distance warms and evaporates and that astronomy is scientific You will never touch the sun or moon, but scientifically you know they are real.. The Sun will light and warm the earth as it rotates and we never question scientifically why. There will be hurricanes, great storms, floods and earthquakes that we can not control nor predict, we have no choice but to accept their existence. We never asked you for blind faith. Simply accept what you understand and then believe in that. You know that the constant is TIME so believe in that. All that you experience in time is real and happens in different dimensions that occur continually. It is impossible to be in more than one dimension as they are continually moving and occurring simultaneously, which in itself may be the variable unknown in the equation in your mind. Such is the nature of TIME and existence. Let us continue to walk and please let me answer any questions that you have. All will be revealed." Donna was processing and could only think to ask, "what about dreams?" Galaxy floated away. A

Different yet equally brilliant colored vision floated up to her and she recognized the sound of her voice to be Sky. Sky spoke melodically and said that dreams can be positive and negative or good and bad. The mind has an infinite filing capacity. Think of a filing room in your brain that holds endless files. When the mind is at rest the files can be misplaced and retrieved randomly. It is not a flawless system, hence the misfiling of memory in the phenomena known as Déjà vu. The brain will file a short term memory into a long term memory file. There is positive and negative in the system. Remember there is no ZERO-SUM. time is always moving as are the dimensions of existence. There are positive and negative forces that work against one another to create balance. That will help you understand scientifically. Donna was stunned with all of the mysteries unfolding in her mind and wanted to speak, but asked Sky to continue. Sky continued, "When you lose one that you love there is trauma in the dimensions due to the overwhelming emotional disruption. If you can understand existence and accept it's simplicity then life and death will challenge you the same as 2+2=4 does. You began with your troubles when you thought you were losing Ben here . Am I correct? "Yes "Donna answered . Sky continued to explain," try to imagine that he did pass on from his present state of life. It may help momentarily for the purpose of this dialogue. The cycle of life and death is natural. Let us think his cycle may have ended , but he is still here with you in another dimension of time. There is a cycle of life and death, but there is no cycle of time. It is the only unexplainable constant and it is everlasting. TIME is the only constant and it is everlasting Sky repeated. We exist in the cycle of life and death just as we exist in the constant movement of time. You exist in both the everlasting, constant of time as well as the cycle of life and death. Scientifically, how can you exist in a cycle that has a beginning and a finality and coexist in a forever moving, everlasting constant? The only possibility to exist in both simultaneously is in different dimensions of the constant, TIME. Do you understand now? . When that concept is clear then the rest is 2+2=4. When the mind is at rest the files of memory are retrieved randomly and as I have explained, it is not a system without flaws. That should clear up dreams for now. They are the mind exploring and existing in time as the mind is at rest. The natural cycle of life and death similarly exists in time as it continues to move on. The past, present and future all exist in time which is constant and always moving just as the earth is rotating right now. They can not exist all at the same time so there are dimensions we can not see. The dimensions are moving in time just as the planet is moving. You can't see it , but know it is happening by the light of the sun. Sky suggested that they stop exploring for now. Donna was pleased as well as exhausted and famished with her revelations. Her running and now her mind working had turned her stomach into a churning furnace that needed fuel. She knew if she continued on in the river walking and thinking she would soon become light headed and dizzy. She needed to sit and eat. First though she asked about Retreat and was told she was off in search of their winter.quarters. The fairies knew Donna was tired and weary so they said goodbye for now and vanished off. Donna called out, "wait! Come back!" Both Galaxy and Sky appeared floating colorfully in front of her again , "can I go over all of what I understand briefly?" Galaxy said, "please do Donna and then go and rest. We are always here for you so you do not have to feel the urgency to settle all of this right now. " Donna reviewed all that she had processed ." We exist in the only constant which is TIME, that is everlasting and always moving as well as the finite cycle of life and death. Both are occurring simultaneously and therefore different dimensions compose our existence in the Universe. We can not exist in both the everlasting constant of TIME and the finite cycle of life and death without the dimensions. Is that an accurate summary? " Very good, you are so very close. It is difficult to see everything in your present state, but you are as close as you can be for now. ", Sky replied and told her to take a rest for now. Donna climbed up over the river bank and helped Ben to jump over the brush and then was off to the blanket she had spread out on the grass. She would share her sandwich and lunch with Ben , but had a ziplock bag with his food in it and emptied it on the blanket for him knowing he must be as famished as she was. She faced the river and took the first bite from her sandwich. Instantly she knew that the cheese was not necessary. It was an expensive, excellent quality cheese, but the pesto was the star of the show so she removed the cheese and fed it to Ben who closed his mouth on it and swallowed like a sea lion does a sardine at an aquarium show. The thoughts of food as she ate the sandwich and BBQ chips moved her to think how great and easy the soup shop choice would have been. Then she thought of the menu for the sales luncheon conference she was hosting tomorrow. She had to do a final review of planning for this important sales meeting which she would do at home. She thought then how insignificant the thoughts of food were as she thought of all of the questions she could have asked her fairy friends. The thoughts of food were comforting in a way that relieved her mind . As she continued to eat she looked at her lower legs and observed the evaporation of the water. It was scientific and proved a good example to her in all that her friends had revealed to her as they conveyed the explanation of existence and its mysteries. She told herself to stop dwelling on the matter and ate until full then let Ben finish the sandwich and chips as she washed down the food with her Sprite soft drink. The questions in her mind were endless. She understood the simplicity of the foundation of existence remembering 2+2=4 just as the only constant was TIME. She needed to process all of the information in her mind. She lay back and gazed up at the sky watching the clouds drift by slowly in time. The sun was above and the earth was rotating as Ben nuzzled up beside her. The forces of nature and time were surrounding her and she had no control or choice. Donna and Ben were part of the all powerful dimension in time as gravity held them to the earth. It was that simple as she understood. That simple for now, but as the constant of time changes so was her place in the dimension subject to change. Ben began to twitch as he fell asleep. Donna continued to watch the clouds as they moved ever so slowly. She wondered about the cycle of life and death. Could Ben have passed through his cycle that day ? Could she have passed through her cycle years ago when her brain was injured? That would mean that her existence had not been as she knew it. Alternate realities, dimensions, dreams? Was this all a dream from another dimension in time? There had to be more. Donna was a Christian and believed in the after life, the mystery of faith and everlasting life in heaven. So how did this new knowledge relate to her faith beliefs? Was there a way to connect the entities or two beliefs together? She felt her mind wandering in circles continuously and wondered as she drifted off to sleep as slowly as the clouds above moved. Ben had moved tightly into her side and her arm was holding him.

CHAPTER 12

Ben had Twitched and fell asleep into the land of dreams. Donna had rapid eye movement and was asleep equally fast. She was in an exhaustive state of unconsciousness dreaming .Donna was back with all three of her lifelong fairy friends now by the river where she first met them as a child. Her childhood friend, Jenny, was there also. Donna asked them what dimension she was in now, as her mind was still consumed by her new revelations. She knew they would have the answer to solidify her thoughts. Galaxy told her she was now in both the past and present because she was in a dream and the relaxed mind could attain both in a dimension. She furthered said, "You are dreaming in the present and have reflected and retrieved a place in time from your past...., you understand this well now." Donna said yes she understood. She began to feel cold. She had been sleeping and had not observed that the earth's rotation had hidden the rays and warmth of the sun behind the mountains and trees. It was not cold enough to force her out of her unconscious state. Donna was walking up the center aisle of St. Mary's church looking at father O'Donnell who was up on the Alter organizing various brass chalice, goblets and trays used during Mass. He heard her footsteps and turned. Happy to see her and also seeing her facial expression he greeted Donna and asked if she needed some help. Donna was a good parishioner and liked him very much. She knew he enjoyed coffee and pastries so she was carrying a box of fresh baked pastries and asked if they could speak in private over coffee and the pastries that she held out for him. He said gladly and they walked over to the Rectory and prepared to sit in a warm, light filled meeting and eating room. Donna explained her feelings and thoughts. Then Donna asked for his insight. He sat thinking deeply and thoughtfully how to respond as they sipped coffee and enjoyed the pastries she arranged on a silver platter from the adjoining kitchen area. It was silent and peaceful as the sun shined through the large double hung windows. Donna fondly respected the stoic look in the clergyman's face as he was thinking and staring at the corner of the room where a statue of the Immaculate Holy Mary stood with her arms open. Donna had spoken freely and told him all that she had experienced. After several minutes of watching father O'Donnell in thought she grew impatient and felt a twinge of guilt, perhaps that was why she she was there. She broke the silence and spoke , "Father, I apologize if I have offended you or the church." He responded , " you have no cause to feel contrite. I was thinking of a way in which to respond to your search." He paused for a moment and began to speak again in an attempt to fulfill her minds expectations, "Donna, the lord is with you on your journey and always..........". Then she felt a movement and heard a sound and her eyes were open. Ben was moving around and playing with John who was sitting next to her. He had moved Ben off the blanket , covered her up and tucked her in. It was well into dusk, not yet fully dark and had grown much cooler as the sun was now shining on another longitude of the earth's axis. Donna looked at her loving husband in his Sheriffs uniform wearing his gun belt and tactical gear and felt safe. She said she had lost track of time. Donna wanted to get up, but pulled the blanket tighter on her and said "Thank you." John bent over and kissed her forehead. He asked, " Are you ok my Love? You have seemed distant." She told him she loved him and said she had so much on her mind regarding work and the conference tomorrow. She would tell him all of the thoughts she was really thinking when she was ready and fully understood everything. For now, she did not want to worry her family. He lay down beside her and touched her as Ben inched in between them. She said they should get home so she could feed the kids, Jack and Emma and check on them He said he picked up pizzas for them and they were doing their homework. She could then prep for her conference and eat some pizza. She asked, " how did you find me?" He said, " I am the Sheriff. I can track and find desperate fugitives . I think I can find my own wife." She loved his playfulness and replied with her own private playfulness , " it's not like I was in a different dimension. ". She put her socks and shoes on, jumped up and kicked him saying , I'll race you and the greyhound here to the car, cmon Ben!" She was off running with Ben trailing as John folded up the blanket an gathered up her lunch remains. He was ready to yell out, "CHEATER!!!!" When he saw her walking back.

CHAPTER 13

He met her half way across the field and then followed her home. They each had a slice of pizza and then Donna opened up her lap top and began reviewing her folder on the luncheon/conference sales meeting. She had reserved the executive banquet room at the Sylvan suites hotel and day spa. The services of the banquet staff were assigned to set up tables and assist with serving, but the food and other services she out sourced to vendors of her choice. She planned meticulously for these sales meetings and invited her best clients. It was an event that demanded leaving a great impression on its attendees, which included her presentation. The list of attendees invited and scheduled to attend were healthcare system hospital directors, medical staff department heads, Medical practice physicians and nurses and pharmacists from the largest pharmacy stores and healthcare systems. The event scheduled to begin at 11am. A pianist was contracted to play lounge and classical favorites in the lobby prior to entering the banquet room. Light fare and hors d' oeuvres were passed in the lobby with champagne cocktails. There was a champagne fountain next to an ice sculpture of the letter B which was the first letter of her company's name, Boone and Boone. The lobby fare included lamb chops with mint jelly sauce, cracked stone crab claws, grilled vegetables and jumbo cocktail shrimp.

In the banquet room tables were along the wall with literature on the newest pharmaceutical treatment medication that her corporation had discovered to treat Alzheimer's, dementia and Parkinson's disease. There were also sample boxes of the pills for the physicians to begin prescribing. Each table had a white rose floral centerpiece that could be taken home by the guests. There was light rock band playing music near the back of the room where a podium was set for her to make her presentation of the newest and greatest discovery at Boone and Boone pharma. There was a spirits cocktails bar set up along the center wall after entering the banquet room. A table with a greeter was set up at the entrance door. The greeter had a master list of attendees to be checked and would give each guest a place card with their table number. The seating arrangement was random to influence mingling, networking and new professional relationships. Donna knew every attendee by name and history and would be mixing throughout the room for the duration of the event. Each seating card had a two digit number on the back. There was a wheel numbered 1-100 on a table next to the cocktail bar. Following Donna's presentation the wheel game would commence. The greeter would take the role of Game host by spinning the wheel and calling out the winning numbers that were the numbers on the back of the seating card. The greeter was a young, jovial and very attractive female sales representative named Dawna. The prizes consisted of all expense paid trips for four-to golf, fishing, casino and spa destinations. This was a five star luncheon that spared no expense. Donna's accounts were very lucrative and she knew how to spend money to make money. There were food stations to further influence moving around the room. There was a Prime rib carving table, ham and Turkey carving tables. There was a fresh rolled sushi station. The staff was assigned to keep the tables clear of used food place settings and flatware so that guests could eat and use table space for devices, lap tops and the literature packages that were given by greeter upon entering. Fresh Lenox plates and flatware could be found at every food station. The atmosphere was intentionally efficient, fluid and productive.

This event was to create and solidify an impression of Donna and her company.

Donna thoroughly reviewed the confirmations of each vendor contracted and then reviewed her presentation which she knew by memory although she would have a tablet with her. Feeling mentally fatigued she closed her folders and and the lap top. She had told John the work was on her mind, but it was not really the dimension of time she thought of. John, Jack and Emma had already gone up to bed and she now found her way up to get some needed sleep. Ben followed her up the stairs. Donna cleared her mind of work and her troubles by thinking about her interaction with her childhood friend Jenny. She imagined that it was not her and Jenny in the river with her fairy friends. That it was her daughter Emma with her sister Shelby. The happy, peaceful thought sent her into a deep sleep. Donna woke early with John. She did not spend time with the kids the day before so intended to this morning. She mixed the batter and began making chocolate/chocolate chip waffles. The smell of the waffles on the iron cooking rose up through the house and they followed the pleasant odor to the kitchen. Their plates were on the island next to butter flavored maple syrup and a half gallon of vanilla ice cream. Jack and Emma went to work immediately on the plates of fresh waffle, they indulged happily with syrup, chocolate and ice cream surrounding their lips. .Now that Donna had a captive audience she could ask them about school and homework.jack asked his mom why the special breakfast on an ordinary school day? She said she had a big day today and wanted to get off to a sweet start as she indulged in the chocolate, syrupy cream. She wasn't certain when she would eat again. She would be occupied walking and talking most of the day so to fuel her body now while she had the time was smart. It was also fun to eat with the kids and talk. John was off to duty. Ben waited on the floor near the island for his chance to taste what his pack was enjoying. It was not his turn and he knew his place in the order. The kids knew mom had a big day ahead of her and Jack said, " you're going to do great mom, love you and thank you." As he got up and went back up to get ready to leave for the school bus Emma said, "yea mom, just what Jack said." Then she followed him up stairs. As she trailed off Donna called, "love you too Emma....."

Donna then made and packed sandwiches for them to take with chips and fruit snacks. Before they could slip by her on the way out she stopped them, gave them their lunch packs and gave them money for ice cream or what ever they chose, hugged them both and told them she loved them , enjoying every moment she had with them in time and the present dimension. She watched them walk out and truly found pleasure in this moment of the cycle of love life and death in time and the present. Then she cleaned up the kitchen and went upstairs to shower and get ready to go. She decided on wearing a black skirt that fell just below the knees with a navy and white striped blouse. It was a professional yet attractive look with low heeled shoes. She did not wear a lot of jewelry. Simple silver hoop earrings that matched her silver necklace with a silver infinity circle charm filled with bright diamonds that John gave to her when they married. She sprayed on her floral scented 'Happy' perfume and was wheeling on her heel to go after checking her light make up in the mirror when something caught her eye. It was a folded piece of paper with her name name on it. She opened it and read it to herself . 'You will be great, love John'. Then she was off with a smile. As she left Ben was in the window watching her as he had done many times with his eyes open and when closed in his dreams. He would wait there for all time if need be. The pack could come back, but he would return to the window and wait for her. There could be no stronger love or loyalty.

CHAPTER 14

Donna left the Jeep at home and drove her white Mercedes S550 coupe. She had it valet parked and walked intently with her black leather lap top business shoulder bag into the lobby. The rented Steinway grand piano was in place with white roses strewn across the lid. Donna paid strict attention to every detail. The classical pianist that she contracted was tickling the Ivories softly playing Tchaikovsky's fantasy overature, Romeo and Juliet. She waved for Julie, the florist to come over. She commented on the fresh roses and asked about the table center pieces. Her true intent was to have a vase placed on the piano lid. The florist had her helper place one as asked immediately. Donna touched the pianist who was dressed in a tuxedo with tails and she said, " that sounds beautiful, you are welcome", she placed a handful of cash into the vase. She intended to encourage others to request selections and dance. The passed fare was to starting to come out as guests arrived. The champagne fountain was flowing and shimmering next to the ice sculpture. A table next to it was for juice mixtures of your choice, orange cranberry, grapefruit and many Waterford crystal flutes. She made her way to the main room to check on the progress and set up. The wiring, screen and laser pointer were in ready for her presentation, set up by the IT personnel of B&B. She knew it was important to check every detail. Her meticulous nature had been a source of her success throughout her life. Could it be now that it was driving her insane in her attempt to understand the nature of the inexplicable? Donna entered the ball room and peered around immediately recognizing the corporation CEO, Robert Boone jr. and the CFO, Michael Reilly walking slowly and reading the presentation research literature she had provided and had instructed to be displayed on the table for attendees to retrieve and review. The two men were reading and talking about the material all the while surveying the room. Donna began to approach the men when she saw something that stopped her and sent a bolt of electricity through her body again from head to toe. To her left she saw father O'Donnell sitting in a chair against the wall also reading her material. She was stopped dead in her tracks. Mr. Boone noticed her and ambitiously waved her over to them. She greeted both men with a hand shake. Boone said he was impressed but not surprised and that they were looking forward to her presentation. He furthered, that she was invaluable to the business. They were anticipating using the filmed presentation to promote their product worldwide. He wished he could offer her further compensation. Reilly interjected and said they would offer greater than the contractual stock options. The profitability of their new medicine would determine the monetary gain. It was reasonable and logically encouraged incentive. The dependability of the options were based on the sales of the new product. Donna thanked them and said providing for her family was her primary concern but there was more. She glanced over at Father O'Donnell and said , "excuse me , I have to see about something." Boone said goodbye, good luck and we will talk later. She approached the priest and said she had planned to come and meet with him. Fr. O'Donnell said that a parishioner who was attending the conference invited him. He is a physician that was trying to help. Fr. O'Donnell said his mother was diagnosed with dementia/Alzheimer's and that the physician/ fellow parishioner said Donna Murphy might be able to help. She reflexively asked, "are we in the same dimension?" He replied automatically, "we are in the Lords dimension." She found ironic humor in the exchange and nervously laughed. Yesterday , in a dream dimension she was seeking his help and today he was seeking help from her. She asked him to review the material and enjoy the presentation and lunch. She asked him to believe what has been proven. The only alternative was to believe in disproving it. Then she excused herself to prepare further. The band was setting up as the workers put the finishing touches on the room. The pianist was playing in the lobby and she felt the buzz in the air. Guests were in and out of the ball room, enjoying the lobby and getting ready for the main event. It was half past noon and she was scheduled to speak at 1pm. She went to the ladies room to look herself over and then stepped outside for a breath of fresh air. She looked up at the sky, thought about her dream as the planet moved on its axis yesterday and then seeing her priest moments ago. Then the conversation with her company's leading officers about the future. The events in her mind were effected by one constant, TIME. Then it was time for her to act. It was her place in the present. She walked to the podium with no introduction needed and began by welcoming everyone and thanking everyone for accepting the invitation. She used her tablet and laser pointer to display diagrams of elements and chemical processes explaining the effects of their break through finding and treatment of a human deficiency. How the human cells, blood and organs reacted to the compounds. She described and highlighted the effectiveness of the new treatment Medicine. Her performance was flawless. The duration of her presentation was approximately 45 minutes. The preparation may have totaled 45 hours. She thanked everyone again and asked that they all enjoy the food, cocktails and music. The band played popular, fun music as Donna made her way through the ball room interacting with every guest.

Donna did not see Father O'Donnell in the room so she went to the double doors and scanned the lobby 360 degrees and found him sitting alone watching the pianist who was effortlessly and brilliantly playing. He was gifted by God with an ear for music and had been playing piano since he was a boy when his mother insisted he take lessons twice a week. The pianist was entertaining himself and others. Father Michael O'Donnell was truly grateful to experience another in such a state of grace. She looked at Fr. O'Donnell and saw a yellow glow of light surrounding him. She thought of pinching herself ,but knew what she was seeing was real so she smiled and asked a staff member to place a chair next to the priest as she walked to the fountain and picked up two crystal flutes and made one Champagne and orange juice and the other champagne and cranberry juice. Donna sat next to Fr. O'Donnell and offered, "mimosa or poinsettia." He chose the OJ. They tapped the Chrystal flutes together in a toast and sipped. She asked if he liked her presentation. He said, "very much so, excuse me for a moment." He handed her his flute and walked to the piano to place money in the glass vase then returned and took his glass thanking her. She said he didn't have to do that to which he replied,"it is the least I could do, listening to you and now him playing has provided me a pleasure that I very much needed."Father Michael O'Donnell was a tall handsome Irish man with a soft tone. He was her favorite person of the parish. His Homily's were well connected to scripture and daily life that touched her. Donna thanked him for being there and offered to help him with his mother. She said that she would call the Rectory to to schedule a meeting so they could meet, have coffee and talk about his mother. The meeting would also present an opportunity for her to explore her thoughts with Fr. O'Donnell. Donna chose to explore her mind and existence scientifically and not betray her faith.

CHAPTER 15

Donna packed a catering box full of fresh carved Turkey and ham with fresh bread to make sandwiches for her family that evening. She had the valet bring her Mercedes up and headed home without delay. Ben was at his Sentinel post in the window. He could somehow sense when she was on her way home. She felt a sense of pride as she drove her luxury sports coupe. She had performed well and was recalling that the CFO, Michael Reilly had offered that there would be stock options. Meaning, when the new medicine hit the market her stock options would most likely double. If the product did well and the corporations stock rose Donna would profit immensely. She was calculating in her mind and was pleased even more so by her performance. Her work compensation was based on sales and performance and she had hit a grand slam today. It could be remembered as a day that set her family to be financially sound for the entirety of their lives. Her thoughts distracted her from all that had consumed her lately. She was enjoying her drive in her magnificent machine which normally stayed in the garage, but she equally enjoyed her Jeep 4x4 and at times much more. The thoughts of money were pleasant as she knew this day could have resulted in millions of dollars for her family. There was more though. John was a Sheriff and never thought of being wealthy. He was a strong willed, honorable man who loved her for richer or poorer. He would be happy for her , but the money wouldn't solve the dilemma in her mind. Fr. O'Donnell was a fly in the ointment she had never anticipated. She was dreaming of visiting with him the day before and today, there he was. She decided to put the thought away and enjoy the victory today. Ben was waiting in the window at his Sentinel post as she wheeled into the drive and felt a great sigh of relief to be home. She unpacked the car with the food, work materials and continued about he day with a bounce in her step enjoying the sense of victory. She made the sandwiches adding mayonnaise to the bread and wrapping them up in fridge for John and the kids when they came home. Donna told John all about her day as he and the kids enjoyed the sandwiches. She felt completely at peace listening to Jack and Emma go back and forth as teenage siblings will do. She could not Love anything more than her children. John was telling her about a fugitive criminal felon that he had tracked , apprehended and brought to justice. She told herself that his sense of accomplishment was equal to her own.

Donna was walking in the direction of the river and a sight shocked her again throughout her entire body . John had his hands around the neck of Tom, the shrink, as he forced his head under water. Donna ran over and yelled , " John stop, you'll kill him." John released his grip and climbed out of the river leaving the body of the lifeless man floating in the river. Donna exclaimed, "John, What have you done?" As she looked and saw Fr. O'Donnell standing on the othe side watching and shaking his head. John asked Donna,"do you know him?" and she said , "not well, his name is Tom, he is a psychiatrist." John told her his name is Phanor Woods and he is not a psychiatrist. He is a schizophrenia committed patient that escaped from the Hardwick Asylum. John said he noticed him by her jeep the other day when he came for her and that he had seen him watching their home. John said he investigated further and determined that he was a dangerous man. Donna asked why he killed him and John pointed and said look,! he killed our little Ben. She looked and saw Ben laying lifeless at the river bank. Donna could not breathe. Her chest felt as if an elephant was sitting on her. She shot straight up and found herself in bed. She breathed in and out relieved that it was a dream. She thought to herself , this has to stop. She nudged John to wake him up. She had to tell him. He woke and asked what was wrong? Donna said she needed to talk and explained her thoughts. He held her and assured her that all was normal. She is a great wife and mother. He said he would help her, but really didn't know how he could. He said, "talk to me when you need to or feel uncertainty. She said it was a long day and they should go back to sleep.

The following day John and the kids were out to work and school. Donna was at the island scrolling through her lap top reviewing the conference invoices and feed back from attendees. Her mind drifted away to her dream last night and what the meaning could be. She recalled Fr. O'Donnell in the dream and her promise to help so she called the Rectory at St. Mary's to schedule a meeting. She thought of the dream and then waking and telling John of her thoughts. He was willing to listen and loved her very much. She continued to believe it was best to work out the mysteries in her mind on her own. She did have to meet with and try to help Fr. O'Donnell. The receptionist asked her to come in tomorrow morning. She gladly accepted. Then before logging off and closing the lap top She read through a well written , gracious letter from Mr. Boone(CEO) and its attachment composed by the CFO, M. Reilly's office that outlined her stock options portfolio and the increases. There were legal clauses and taxation disclaimers. Donna understood all of the data quite simply. Her scientific mind was concerned and annoyed by existence not money so she called for Ben who was sitting by the door as if he was reading her mind. She grabbed his leash and said, "as you wish my gentle Ben, let's go." Off they went in the jeep. She didn't pack or plan to have lunch. Donna had a theory to test . The dream of the night before had unsettled Donna. Subsequently, listening to the words coming out as she explained to John her thoughts and their relevance to the dream moved her to think once more that it would sound to others as though she was losing her mind. Donna drove about two miles with Ben on the front passenger seat peering around. He then stared at her knowing they were not at the park. Donna pulled off the road into a gravel parking area between the road and a tree line. There were other vehicles with moderate traffic of people with fishing rods, nets and tackle boxes coming from and going to a trail opening in the tree line that winded through the woods to a river. Donna leashed Ben in order to stop him from straying off the trail and into the dense tree filled woods. She had a goal to get close to the river. Donna was wearing her Merrill terrain shoes and navigated the mild trail with ease. In minutes she could see the river ahead of her. When she arrived at the river bank there were people fishing along the bank north and south as well as in the river wearing rubber waders. It was a peaceful setting. She had nothing in common with the anglers. She was not there in search of river trout. She was seeking answers to the Unknown. In her dreams and thoughts she had met with and interacted with her colorful, floating fairy friends. They had imparted wisdom and knowledge. Donna wanted to test their existence by searching for them ina different, random place. As the anglers cast and searched for trout she walked along the bank scanning for her friends. She could see the shadows of trout that seemed to be still, but they were swimming against the current. Donna tried to put aside her thoughts of existence. She had a great success the day before. As she strolled by the river bank she told herself , if it ain't broke don't, don't fix it. The nightmare of a dream the night before pushed her probing , scientific mind and she had to test existence at a different river. It might prove nothing. . It was worth a walk in the woods. .she watched her little Ben running up and down the path beside the river. The playful Benji/Toto morkie mix looked back to his master and she smiled and called out to him, "this is all your fault you know, you and your dreams Ben." She had walked far enough away from the anglers, but still felt foolish talking to her Ben alone in the woods. Donna called for Ben to follow as she spun on her heel to turn back. Ben was charging back to her on the path and the harp like sounding voice called out, "Donna, stop him." She followed the sound and then could see the three magnificent colors floating like humming birds above the brush at the bank of the river. Donna put her arm out signaling for Ben to stop and he slid directly beside her. She was preparing to speak and Retreat started before she could get a word out. "It is good to see you again Donna, I told you we would always be here for you." Donna replied, " yes and I believe you. I needed to test myself I suppose. My question is, why am I here? Did something traumatic happen in my mind ? Was it my surgery long ago? The death of Alex and the near death of my little Ben? I understand my existence and wonder if I should."

Galaxy spoke, "It is what you chose. You want to be here. You are very gifted. You choose your existence in time. Most can not , but you are special. Donna said, " I was happy and felt sound where I was. Can I go back?" Sky then buzzed up to her ear and spoke, "you can choose, we will always be here. It is not the place as you have learned." Then Retreat broke in, "it is good that you came here. Now you Can see it is in you." Donna felt an emotional rush surge through her and felt a tear well in her eye. Ben could feel the emotion and pushed her leg with his head. Retreat said, "gentle Ben is telling you to go,". "Go Donna and we will see you again." She set off back on the path with Ben and turned at the trail back to her Jeep. She was now eager to get on with life. She went directly to the market and purchased all she needed to make dinner for her family. She wanted to feel as she had in the past. She thought of times in the past and the feelings of happiness. Yes, she thought , the constant movement of time prohibits the return to dimensions. She could find that happiness in a new dimension if she chose to.

Donna unpacked the Jeep and Ben settled on his bed by the kitchen as she started preparing the food. He always watched her when she cooked. The smells stimulated him. First she brought the tomato gravy to a simmer and then cut up the chicken and eggplant before dredging and frying it slice by slice. Then she shredded fresh cheeses. Everything was layered in a deep baking pan and placed in the oven. Donna sliced a loaf of semolina bread for making sandwiches or dunking in the tomato gravy. She shredded fresh Parmesan cheese and set the table. The house smelled like home. When John and the kids came home they were each smiling to smell the aroma of home cooking. Donna took John aside and said she was doing good and the thoughts she had were all gone. He replied that he loved her no matter what and she could tell him anything, at any time. Dinner was ready and they sat to eat together. John opened a good bottle of red wine for Donna and himself. They all ate until full and were happy. Donna felt like she was in the perfect place in time. She made a plate for Ben that he did not hesitate to lick clean. That is why he enjoyed watching her cook. He knew as a member of the pack his turn would come to eat the same food and it was better than the other food. Everyone slept well that night. They all slept in , but Donna recalled her call to the Rectory and had to get up and get ready.

CHAPTER 16

Donna showered and dressed in a business casual outfit, white slacks with a floral print white blouse. She stopped at pagano's bakery and picked up a box of pastries then off in her white Mercedes sports coupe to the Rectory. She met Fr. O'Donnell in the room that had been in her dream. This was in the present time and dimension. He Thanked her for coming and she opened her bag to retrieve the literature from her presentation and sample boxes of the medicine. She opened the pastry box on the table as he poured two cups of coffee. There was cream and sugar on the table and she mixed her coffee with a splash of cream. He said he had read through the material and then explained that the fellow parishioner that recommended that he use his invitation to the presentation. was Dr. John O'Connor. He said he had asked Dr. O'Connor for advice regarding his mother and that he was told that you are the one who could help. "Dr. O'Connor said you are brilliant and after watching your conference I agree. Do you think you Can help me? Rather my Mom?"

Donna smiled and said, "I thought of coming to you for help, how ironic. I am not a medical Doctor. I can tell you how the medicine can help." Donna explained how the cholinestase enzyme inhibitors increased hemoglobin in the affected red blood cells in the brain of someone with Alzheimer's and or Parkinson's disease. The medicine seeks the cells and molecules and attaches to them fitting specifically and precisely to alter, interfere with abnormalities by leveling the blood cells. She pointed out the elements in a diagram that she drew while explaining. Then a thought occurred to her which she did not reveal. It bothered her and she buried it in her mind to retrieve another time. She assured him that she had every confidence that the medicine would support his mother's mental health and clarity. She said she could not prescribe the medicine and Dr. O'Connor could, but she would leave him with the box of sample pills and wrote down the cycle recommended dosage. As they finished their coffee and danish he asked why she had wanted to meet prior to his asking her for help. Donna was not certain if she wanted to open that door again. She trusted him and as she sipped her coffee she thought, why not? Donna asked, " is it normal for a Christian to have thoughts of a parallel universe or dimensions? He thought for a moment of the questions origin coming from such a brilliant scientific persons mind. He said, "we live in God's universe in which there are many dimensions. God chooses yours." Donna was satisfied and she thanked him for his time and said she would be of further help if needed, wishing him blessings for his mother and then departed.

Donna walked around to the back of the church and was ready sit at the bench next to the marble monument, but walking and thinking would be more productive so she continued around the church and over to the town square, or better known as 'the green' to walk . It was a clear , quiet morning with few people around perfect for walking and pondering with no interruption. She thought of John, Jack and Emma making eggs and eating a late breakfast. Then her mind returned to the place it went sideways . When she explained how the red blood cells were affected by the enzyme cholinesterase she thought she went too deep in the woods for Fr. O'Donnell and it was confirmed by the blank look on his face. But, it also reminded her of its other uses in treatment for poisoning by arsenic and in treatment of paralysis. What similar enzymes could be used to treat brain cells in a case like hers? She was living in different dimensions of time and existence. Should she be satisfied with her philosophical explanation from her fairy friends and her mystery of faith parallel as explained by her clergy friend. Why not let it be? Something still was bothering her and she was making herself crazy. Her friend and colleague Nancy came to her mind. Nancy Nemeth was the Senior Laboratory researcher and scientist at Boone and they had worked together on new medicines in the past. Donna collaborated on the research and then found gratification in selling the ideas. She would call Nancy on Monday to set up a time to bounce ideas around. She trusted Nancy. Until then she would enjoy her victory at the luncheon. Time to get back home. That was enough thinking for today.

CHAPTER 17

Donna walked back to her car parked in the parking lot between the Rectory and the church. She looked at her phone that she in its holder and saw missed call and Urgent message from John. She called immediately and he said come home right away, it's Ben , I think he's gone. She hung up and sped out of the parking lot wondering what gone meant. Lost run away, dead? She drove her Mercedes like a grand prix car in the streets of Italy. Until she spun into the drive and ran into the house. John said, "I'm sorry honey, he's dead ", and pointed to wear Ben lay on his bed. She ran and picked him up and then back out to the car. John was calling, " Donna, he's gone." She ignored him and pulled out again. With Ben laying on the front seat she drove with one arm on him and the other on the wheel. She gathered herself, taking deep breaths and drove more carefully. No sense in her or anyone else dying now. She pulled into the parking lot of the Veterinarians office. She carried Ben inside and told the receptionist this was an emergency. She carried Ben right in to an exam room. The Vet, Dr. Belmont came in and said, "Mrs. Murphy, I am so sorry." He was touching Ben and listening with a stethoscope. Donna spoke, "I thought you said he was fine after the test results." The Vet said, " no, I said he was incurable, you should take him home and love him, he doesn't have much time left." She grabbed Ben to pick him up as she cried and the Vet helped her wrap him in a blanket saying he was so sorry, " you must be in shock." She thought, What is happening as she thanked him and carried Ben to the car. She could not go straight home. She was utterly distraught and confused. She did a search of psychiatrists in the area and found a Thomas Snyder. She called asked to come in for an emergency appointment after reminding him she was the woman from the park. He agreed to see her so she set out for his office. She pulled up to the address and it was a classic Tudor style home with meticulously landscaped gardens with a burning gas lamp post at both of the walk ways. One led to an entrance that had an office sign on a post. Donna parked in the drive and proceeded to the office door. It was a round top wooden door that was open. The screen door provided a view inside. There was a sitting area and another door the opened to an office. She called inside and was told to come in. She entered and proceeded to the office and sat across from Tom, shaking hands and exchanging greetings. Donna said she wanted to ask him a few questions. She said she was not crazy, but wanted to know if he recalled her in the park with her dog. He looked stunned. He replied that he saw her one day walking with her dog and then again by the river talking to herself and she denied it, that is why he asked if she needed to talk. Donna felt sick and thought she might be having a nervous breakdown so she apologized for intruding and said she had to go. She hurried to her car and looked at Ben in the blanket in the front seat and drove home sobbing quietly. She thought for sure she was having a breakdown and needed to be home. She pulled over because she could not breathe. She felt someone gabbing her shoulders and pulled her arms up. John was shaking her and talking. He said, "Donna, baby, wake up, you said you were meeting with Father O'Donnell today." She grabbed him and hugged him hard. He said you were having a bad dream baby, wake up. She asked desperately, "where is Ben?" He said down stairs with the kids most likely eating eggs. She asked him to call the Rectory and say she was not feeling well. No problem he would take care of it. She pulled the blanket tight over her body and called out for Ben who came charging and jumped on the bed nuzzling into her neck and reaching up up to lick her tears. She would call herself to reschedule, right now she needed to sleep in peace. When she woke hours later she called and scheduled to meet father O'Donnell on Monday. John asked to speak with her. They went outside in the yard. John suggested to Donna that if she needed some help with her thoughts that he would support her. She grew upset, "you think I am crazy?" John backed off apologetically, "No no never I love you. I think you are going through a hard time. Maybe , you need to get away." This threw gasoline on a fire. "You want to send me to a mental clinic, a sanatarium?" Donna began to cry, "John, I'm not crazy!!!" He grabbed her hands, "No, no no, I meant a get away, the Grand Canyon."he hugged her tightly and said " I will help you." Donna said, " let's drop it. John." John said, " think of a place you would like to go. You just feel better, I'll support you. I have another idea Donna," he finished saying with a sly, yet innocent smile. She smiled , kissed his lips and said, "you best not be thinking of the funny farm for me Sheriff Murphy." John grabbed her , "Never!"

CHAPTER 18

On Monday Donna met with Father O'Donnell and their discussion was nearly identical to the events in her dream. Following the meeting, unlike in her dream she did not go for a walk to think. There was no urgent call from John. Donna made a call to her friend and colleague, Nancy Nemeth. Donna said she would like to discuss something with her . Nancy said that Donna was the buzz of the company since her presentation and the release of their newest medicine that hit the market. Nancy said she was in the Lab at Boone headquarters and asked Donna to come and visit her now if she chose to. Donna told her she was on her way.

Donna had full access and palm scanned her way through the man trap security access door. Nancy was in a lab coat at a table studying over drawings, graphs and equations. She waved Donna over pulled a stool close to her own. Donna sat and said,"I hope it isn't a bad time." Nancy said ,"Not at all. I would ask you to review some boring experiments, but I think you have something else on your mind. Is it good or bad?" Donna said, "thoughts I want to talk about. I respect your knowledge and opinions." Nancy said, "sounds good, very interesting, please do tell."Donna explained her thoughts and questioned the brain cells and blood cells. Is it possible to alter our medicine that would level the brain to view the world in one dimension?" She was thinking out loud, rambling and revealing her thoughts until Nancy stopped her. Donna, "you are the most intelligent, level headed human that I have ever known Why don't we look at this from the opposite direction? Outside in , not inside out?" Donna said, " go on…". Silence for a moment as they both looked at each other as if they were solving a puzzle. Nancy said ," I want you to humor me and be a subject of something I have been developing." Nancy opened a drawer in the table and retrieved a sample kit. Donna was curious,"what is this?" Nancy replied,"humor me, let me swab your mouth?" She swapped saliva from Donna's mouth and then said she would run it through a new screening process. "I developed a new chemical test for employers. It isn't approved yet." Donna chuckled,"you think I'm on drugs? My husband thinks I'm cuckoo, what next? An exorcism?" Nancy said, " just humor me. Outside /In , two heads are better than one." Ok ok go,Donna said.

Nancy came back five minutes later and said, "remember when I asked good or bad when you came in? Well, the good is, I think scientifically as you do and agree with every thought you have on existence, time, dimensions and dreams. The bad is, there are traces of Diethylamide, Lysergic acid in your cells." Donna's jaw dropped, "I have been drugged?"Nancy said, "the traces are miniscule. I ran it through the program twice to be absolutely positive. It must have happened three weeks ago. It is an acid that affects the brain cells stimulating abstract thoughts and hallucinations ." Donna asked, more rhetorically thinking to herself, "but how?, Well I'm not crazy, that's good news, but how?" Nancy said, "talk to your husband." Donna was stunned, "you think John would do this to me?!" Nancy said, "No, no, I met John, the Sheriff, he could investigate and figure out how." Donna laughed and hugged Nancy saying, "Thank you Nancy, you are forever a friend for all time, existence and in every dimension. Please keep this between us, I should go." Nancy hugged her and said, "love you, when you are ready give up swanky parties and all that money, come be with me in the Lab." Donna chuckled and waved goodbye as she exited the Lab and the Headquarters with her mind set on going straight home.

CHAPTER 19

When she parked in the drive and opened the car door she could hear the barking and yelping inside. It grew loud and out of the ordinary as she approached the mud room door. Ben never sounds like this she thought. What is going on in there. She opened the door and could hear chaos. John was standing at the island smiling. Jack and Emma were talking loudly as the barking and yelping grew louder. She followed the sound around to the living room and heard John say, "surprise honey." She saw Ben fighting off a tiny version of himself jumping and nipping at his jowls. She called to him and he ran to her for relief and help. The little puppy slid and chased after him. She reached down and touched Ben . Then she picked up the morkie, also known as a Morkshire(Maltese/Yorkshire terrier mix)puppy, the same as Ben and said,"who are you?" John had moved by her side and put his arm around her. "Honey, she is yours." Donna held up the puppy, a small, female version of Ben and asked, "why?" John continued, "I wanted to surprise you, to help. I said I had another idea. You have been so upset since Ben got sick. Ben will feel young again with a puppy in his pack. Your mind will be more at ease , I hope. All you have to do is name her now." Donna said, " that's is easy, her name is Shelby." Donna hugged the puppy and put her down to go play with Ben. John asked, "why Shelby?" She did not hesitate, "I always loved that name. If we didn't have an Emma, I could have had a daughter named Shelby." The words sent a chill through her.

She cleared her mind and asked, "can we take them to the park, me and you? There is something I need to talk to you about." John said let's go. Off in the Jeep they went. At Ramapo state park they decided to start with a leash on both and then to let the dogs play in the field. Tom, the shrink, was in the parking area next to his car. He called over to say hello to Donna and ask how she was feeling. Donna, John and the dogs went off to the path and John asked who that man was. Donna told him that Tom is a man that walks in the park and had talked to her in the past. John made a mental note of Tom's vehicle registration number. Then he asked what she wanted to talk to him about. She told him of the discovery she had made when she met with Nancy earlier . John was stunned. He said nothing for a few minutes as they guided Ben with the new puppy, Shelby. Then he stopped at the field adjacent to the path. He said, "let's turn them loose to play." Ben ran off to chase his adversaries, birds and squirrels, with his new adversary nipping at his heels. Ben circled out in the field and began to confront the puppy. They rolled, played and nipped at each other. John said, " look how young Ben looks again. I thought this would be good for YOU and him. I still think we need to go away on a trip." Donna was smiling happily watching the dogs play. John asked, " now, tell me more about this drug you have been slipped. I Have to conduct an investigation."

Donna told him what the acid chemical was. He asked who she suspected. She said she honestly did not know, but subconsciously looked in the direction of the parking area and John noticed. She wanted to change the subject for now and said she was very happy with Shelby and thanked him for his thoughtful surprise. The puppy was wearing Ben down with her endless energy and passion, happy to be in her new pack. Ben came walking back to Donna slowly as he was exhausted. Donna knew he wanted to go home. He never looked so tired when on walks and runs, but he was happy. The puppy was also tired following his lead. They went back to the Jeep and talked about taking a few days off to go away. The dogs and kids were going too. John asked questions about Nancy and others at Boone thinking of suspects and motives. Donna knew it and her own mind was working on the same questions. Donna's mind was quickly moving through names and faces like it was a slide show. She felt a tinge of guilt when John and Nancy were thought of. She turned off the thoughts when they were driving home. She told John she was going to plan a road trip to the Grand Canyon. They could hike down the canyon and stay overnight at the luxury lodge near the Colorado river. He said, "that sounds like a great idea. When we get home I will contact the major crime detective unit and we will find out who'd committed this heinous act." Donna tried to take her mind off the subject, but when he said he was ready to start investigating immediately she felt responsible. After all, she was the one who initiated the subject. She couldn't help but think of who had done this to her and why. Then she thought of what little she knew about hallucinogenic acid and it occurred to her that there was the possibility of relapses. How much was really known scientifically about the effects of hallucinogenic acid on the cells in the brain? She could talk to Nancy about that later. Then she thought of Nancy and her remark of coming to work in Lab. No way Nancy could do this. Then to John, no way he could. These thoughts made her equally or more uncomfortable than anything that had she had been confused by. She believed in what she was thinking about existence. She could not face the thought that one she loved would do something to hurt her. She turned to look at the dogs lying on the back seat close together and exhausted. It made her feel happy as they arrived at home. Shelby began following Ben around and he was slowly beginning to like it as he looked for her behind him.

CHAPTER 20

The following day life resumed as if it had always been this way. John was off to work and kids at school. The dogs were sharing the bed that was Bens. He came down with John and the kids and settled in with Shelby on his bed. Donna logged in on her lap top to check her accounts and give attention to clients via emails and attachments. She scrolled through communications and thought of John at work investigating the allegation she made. She thought of how difficult it might be to confirm an allegation as such. Should she try to solve her own problem? John was trained and experienced, but this was an allegation by her based on a friends test. She continued to write to clients and respond, all the while wondering if she should pursue the search further herself of who drugged her. She logged off and called for Ben. A walk with Ben and his new adversary in the park was a better idea right now. She led them to the Jeep and off they went. Donna made a stop at Al's soup and sandwich shop. She picked a white bean escarole soup and tuna fish sandwich combo with an orange and a bottle of Sprite. Back in the Jeep she wondered how someone could have drugged her. Most beverages she drank were sealed except for the times that she ordered coffee so that narrowed down the possibilities. She always watched her coffee being poured and mixed to see that it was done correctly. She was a non-self avowed perfectionist. John and her children were the only ones that she could think of that could possibly have slipped her something. The thought made her shudder and feel sick. How could she think such thoughts? She wished she was insane. Rather it be me than my family.

She wheeled into the park and found a spot to park. The dogs were up and excited, jumping about and looking out the windows eager to run free. Donna grabbed her bag with the lunch and let the dogs out unleashed. She told Ben to stay near and pointed to her side. It was the perfect time to teach the younger Shelby by example. Donna pulled the blanket out and saw the large Evian water bottles. She subconsciously noticed they were all sealed with new caps. Then she heard a familiar voice call out to her. She turned her head and saw Tom , the psychiatrist, waving over to her. She waved back. Still with the thought of water bottles in her mind, then the sight of Tom she thought of motive. Why would someone want to drug her? It was obviously, not to kill her. The dogs were itching to run and play. Let it go she thought to herself. Before she started off she thought the bag and blanket were too cumbersome. She put them in the back of the Jeep and took one leash in the event that the puppy was not capable yet of obedience. She could come back to get lunch or take it home. That would be dictated by the dogs' behavior. Donna commanded the dogs stay by her side and walked to the path. When on the path that looped around the field she let them run off in the grass to play. Ben was seeking the birds and squirrels and the puppy followed near to him. Donna was pleased to see her following in his ways. It was a good idea she thought. Ben was looking like a young dog again and Donna had her mind on something new. It was a pleasant distraction. The distractions had changed for Donna though. What was once existence had evolved into the cause of her previous thoughts. Ultimately, she knew it was best to focus on the dogs. Mean while, Ben and Shelby were chasing down their enemies in the field as Donna strode along the path. Tom called out from behind her and she slowed to allow him to catch up. He had been kind and polite to her. She felt no cause to be rude to him. He walked up beside her and asked how she was feeling. "fine," she replied, lying, she was feeling uncertain about him, but could not say that. He said he was happy to see her feeling well and liked her new puppy. Then asked, "was that your husband with you the other day?" Donna said, " yes his name is John Murphy and our new little girl there is Shelby." Pointing to the dogs.he then asked if they had children. He was intruding, making her feel as she did at a previous interaction so she asked a question of her own. "Yes we do, is your office in your home?" She felt pleased at her response, thinking of her dream and his office attached to a Tudor home. She could be completely off , after all it was a dream. He hesitated thinking how could she know? He replied, "Yes, how did you know?" Now she hesitated feeling happy to put him on his heels. It was a guess from a dream. She would never tell him why. Let him think. Donna said nothing and walked thinking, it was coincidence. Half way around the loop the dogs came running. They were ready to be back with their pack leader. She made them follow her across the field back to the car to get lunch and the blanket. Ben knew what was happening and Shelby followed , learning. Back at the Jeep, Donna first poured some water in a dog bowl she had in the back of the Jeep. Then she gave them milk bones from the box she had for times like this. There was a picnic style table across the field off the path, near the river shaded by trees. She decided to eat lunch there so she grabbed the bag and blanket and headed over with the dogs trailing. She spread the blanket over the table and unpacked the lunch from Al's. Donna ate the soup and half of the sandwich. She was fully satisfied and wanted to take a walk up the hill to look at the old mine ruins and the bird sanctuary. The last time there she was spooked and wanted to prove to herself it was nothing. She would not live in fear or be paranoid. She left her lunch on the table, bottle of Sprite with the safety seal broken. She called her dogs to follow and never looked back as she hit the path and then turned up the hill. She refused to be a victim or prisoner of fear. She told herself what happened is in the past. It could have been a mistake or mistaken identity. She also could not live in denial for that matter either. The knowledge she gained relating the constant , zero sum of TIME and existence entered her mind as she was approached the crest of the hill. Her stomach was full and she felt slightly out of breath. The old mine ruins were on her right. She turned to approach for a closer look. Ben paused and Shelby followed his lead. She said, "cmon you cowards," jokingly and they hesitantly followed as they stared into the black unknown of the cavern. Donna stopped at the opening and also stared into the blackness as her thoughts drifted to existence and time. She would not be a victim, as her mind wandered, staring into the blackness. If she was in the present and existence occurred simultaneously than could she enter the past in her present state or for that matter the future. She recalled her conversation with Father O'Donnell. He had not disputed her view of existence. He did add that the Universe was God's creation and we were all part of it. She continued in thought. It was impossible for her scientific mind to comprehend that life could be random. In the Universe the earth revolves around the sun providing light and infinite life forms. The plants, the tides of the seas all provided life. All matter existed by design. The complexity of life and matter deemed it impossible to be random. Therefore, her conclusion and understanding of existence was proven. She broke her gaze and looked down at the dogs and smiled at their existence . They perceived dimensions differently and reasoned differently. There were limitations for them and for her. She reasoned that she could not enter different dimensions in time simultaneously. She was staring again into the dark cavern. Donna concluded only when she transitioned from her present state would it be possible to exist in all of time Then she broke free from her gaze and turned on her heel heading back up the hill, the dogs following, to its summit where it opened to a meadow and trees ideal for watching birds.

At the top Donna walked on a trail, similar to that off a game trail made by animals in the brush. This was a trail made by humans that adventured circling the meadow. The dogs ventured off into the meadow in search of other critters and creatures that they sensed were present. Donna looked up at the sky and the sun was fading over the horizon slowly as the earth moved and the law of gravity held her and the dogs tightly to its surface. She could not help but fixate on a great bird of prey soaring lower in flight. It was an Eagle with a large fish held in its powerful Talons. The bird of prey, also known as Raptor, soared low from high in the sky and landed in a tree where its nest was, to presumably feed its young. She stared in awe thinking that such grace and majesty of life was not happenstance. She felt an immense surge of energy and love of life, that her mind washed clean of any confusion. She felt suddenly hungry again. She thought, thinking intensely makes me hungrier than exercising. She clapped and called for Ben and Shelby whom responded and emerged from the brush in the meadow momentarily. They were off and descending the hill. Donna and her two best friends. She knew Love was the reason for Shelby and she loved Ben with all of her heart. But, Shelby was beginning to notch a place in her heart as well. With her new found energy, appetite and zest for life came a thought that shocked her body through and through as she bounced down the hill with her loyal and loving companions by her side. Never second guess your yourself and what you know to be true. Tomorrow will always come just as the earth will continually revolve and the sun will shine. TIME is the constant. Her thoughts were solidified. She sat at the table, opened and finished her sandwich sharing pieces with Ben and Shelby. She opened and washed down her sandwich with the Sprite soft drink never giving a thought to what could be in it. She wrapped everything up to take to the refuse receptacle and they were off across the field to the parking area.

CHAPTER 21

When Donna and the dogs arrived back at the Jeep Tom was standing by his car drinking a bottle of water. Evian water she noticed. He asked her, "Mrs. Murphy, how could you know where I work and live?" Donna felt a pit in her stomach, but felt she deserved it. She did leave him with a dangling carrot, so felt she deserved the jab. She lied, " I have never given it a thought." He was fast, "my offer still stands, if you need to talk you are welcome to come in to my office, which is at my home." Donna thanked him and said no. She was feeling so good and could not help herself from quipping, "that is my favorite water." Then she waved goodbye, jumped in the Jeep with the dogs and was on her way home. John and the kids were already eating. She offered to make something for dinner. They were very happy eating baked Red Baron frozen pizza and declined. Donna was still satisfied from her lunch and was relieved that dinner was not necessary. John told Donna he was working on the case. There were only sporadic and rare arrests for (LSD). Donna did not want to talk about the subject with the kids home. She said she needed to make a work call and went outside. Donna called Nancy at the lab. John felt uneasy and watched Donna on the phone outside. Donna asked Nancy questions about Lysergic acid(LSD). How to obtain it and its uses. Nancy told her it had to be made. It was not approved for any use. A scientist created it accidentally many years ago when experimenting on animals. It was tried with humans for psychological disorders, schizophrenia, depression etc and then with military personnel for PTSD(post traumatic stress disorder) and other classified experiments. It was never approved for treatment in medicine. It was leaked to the population and used recreationally. It has been for many decades and is still illegal. The legality prompted Donna to tell Nancy that John was looking into the matter with nothing yet. Donna then told her that she left her food and drink unattended at the park and that a suspicious fella was there. She said it was not a trap. She wasn't doubting what she thought and believed, it was a subconscious decision. Nancy's voice grew urgent, "Donna, DO NOT take matters into your own hands please! Let John do what he can. ". Donna said, "you are right, thanks Nance, bye."Donna began to walk back inside and saw John looking out through the window. John asked if all was ok. She said of course I and that she was working on their plans to get away.

The following day Donna told Ben and Shelby to have fun and keep each other company, that is why they are together. They were already thick as thieves on the sofa together. Donna was off in her Mercedes to an address she could see in her mind, 724 Cross Avenue. She saw it as she did in a dream. When she arrived there it was precisely as her dream, the Tudor home with the office shingle hung by the annex. There was a familiar metallic blue Jaguar in the drive near the office. She continued on driving, thinking what am I doing here and how do I know that car? She turned left at the four way and drove to the next street then left again at the three way circling back to cross Avenue. She slowed to a slow crawl at intersection of Cross Ave. and looked to the left. Donna saw John's unmarked police vehicle parked in front of the home. At that instant she remembered that Nancy drove a metallic blue Jaguar. She looked and saw John talking to Nancy as Tom approached and joined them. Donna felt frozen, numb until a loud sound shook her, jolting her body. Her arms flew upward and her head snapped. She reacted mentally from her state of shock seeing the car behind her in the rear view mirror that loudly sounded the horn. Donna drove forward slowly, hoping instinctually not to be observed with an influx of thoughts racing through her mind. Not knowing what to think or do , she decided not to say or do anything. Donna went to the path adjacent to the river to walk and watch the anglers in the water playing catch me if you can with the river trout. The anglers looked at peace matching wits with their prey. It was not a zero sum contest, where as with the Raptor it was life and death, not a peaceful game. The young birds needed to eat. The instinct of the Eagle was to watch , wait and then strike. It could not fail. Donna walked along the path watching the peaceful game of the angler and thinking of the Raptor. She was at peace until she thought of her role in in the zero sum game of life. Who was watching her as the Raptor and why? Why was John with Nancy? Was that really what she saw? How could she know where Tom lived and worked? She tripped on a tree root that was above the earths surface and caught herself. She knew that trees near a river had roots above the surface because she had several river birch tees on their property. It jarred her back to the present as the car horn sound did. She was slightly mad at herself, but focused. She remembered she was in the present held to the earth by gravity and time was not a zero sum game. She needed to forget the thoughts. It would not resolve problems, but it would make her insane, which she knew she was not. She walked along listening to the sounds of the forest and watching the water ripple and flow slowly. She thought of an exercise that she was taught when young. Close your eyes and listen. Try to hear all of the sounds that normally you would not hear. She sat down on a patch of grass and closed her eyes, listening. The exercise had taken her mind off of everything and it amused her. She could hear the sounds of vehicles off in the distance, tree limbs whining as they rubbed in the subtle breeze and insects buzzing quietly. Donna was startled by a voice. The voice of a man. She opened her eyes and a man in uniform was standing before her. He was speaking cold and directly, "ma'am, ma'am, are you ok?" Her first thought was John had someone following her. She looked at the patch on the uniform that read Fish and Game. She began to chuckle, thinking 'no , no I'm being paranoid. '. She stood up and put out her hand, "it's Mrs. Murphy, Donna Murphy, call me Donna, and yes I'm fine, just resting." The smiling, kind eyed, handsome man shook her hand and said,"I am James Johnson, wild life officer, you can call me Jim." He then asked, "do you have a fishing license Donna?" She could not help her laughing. She felt happy and amused, "fishing? I'm not fishing, I am the fish." Jim found her happy laughter contagious and smiled, chuckled, but steadied him self. " Donna, is someone following you, what do you mean you are the fish?" Donna gathered herself and said," no, I hope not, I have been thinking too much." He said, " pardon me for saying this and I mean no offense or disrespect, but you are far too pretty to be walking out in the woods alone." She said, "I'm not offended, Thank you for your concern and kind words, perhaps I should go. I find it peaceful watching people fish in the river." She moved on her heel letting go of his hand and was beginning to walk away when he called out, "Donna are you sure your ok?" With a questioning look on his face and one raised eyebrow. Donna was still smiling and chuckling to herself as she muttered, not really, if you see three fairies by the river bank let me know. She thought to herself, ' YOU ARE INSANE, go home Donna'. Jim called out, "this area is patrolled so you can feel safe here, see you again, good luck." She went home and played with the dogs outside. That night John asked about her day and said he was still working on the investigation into LSD in the area. Donna said nothing and was configuring a plan in her mind.

CHAPTER 22

The following day Donna routinely checked her responsibilities at work and nothing struck her as urgent. Money account transfers from clients and product invoices were satisfactory. Contract renewals were calendar based and she had them scheduled so they were aligned for renewal in December each year. Clients that requested quarterly contracts were in a separate folder. All were easily tracked. It was an ordinary day. She had her own plan and packed up the dogs and needs . Ben and a Shelby were excited and jumped in the Jeep. Donna had no plans on running or eating lunch today. She was going fishing today. Her plan was to be the eagle for now on. She drove to the park and let the dogs out to run free. Shelby was learning fast by the side of her Mentor, Ben leading her. Donna looked around for Tom ,'the Shrink' and he was no where around. She walked on the loop path and watched the dogs running in the field. She could see that the puppy grew tired and frustrated chasing birds and squirrels. It amused Ben watching the puppy try her best. He was once like her, now she was a member of the pack so he stayed close by her. When she stopped to rest and sat down he nipped and nudged her affectionately. It was his method of encouragement. On the final stretch of the loop Donna looked at the river and saw nothing. Twenty five or so minutes had elapsed and she was back at the parking lot. She thought, just my luck. The one day I want to see the quack and he isn't here. She smiled at the irony. This would not stand. She was hunting and fishing. She googled his name and psychiatrists and found the number for Thomas Snyder, P C on cross avenue. She must have looked it up previously and forgotten. It did not matter, she called the number and he picked up quickly. She thought, he must have caller ID. "Hello Tom , this is Donna Murphy, is this a bad time?" "No Donna, Can I help you?" Donna said, "perhaps, a colleague of mine needs help. "her name is Nancy Nemeth, are you familiar with that name?" Tom replied, "no , sorry, never heard that name, should I have." Donna continued , "No, there must be a mistake, she is my colleague and friend and I thought you were treating her." "No Donna I can't discuss patients, but that name is not familiar to me." She said goodbye and hung up thinking she botched that. Wrong line of questioning. He told her nothing and she exposed her curiosity. Bad fishing today. She called to the dogs and they were there ready for water and snacks, so she rewarded them. She thought,' got nowhere today but it will come.' She knew she was no quitter and would succeed. Donna knew she was not naturally a hunter, she was a gatherer, gatherer of facts and problem solving, a scientist , not an investigator. Maybe best idea was to take a break after her first attempt to set a snare and coming up empty. Donna did not like to fail. She focused on a different problem. Donna motioned for her companions to follow and walked back off across the field to the river. . Ben and Shelby had water and milk bone snacks and were reinvigorated as they followed her across the field loyally and happily. Donna looked back and felt entirely grateful to John. She felt like Dorothy, the Wizard of Oz, with two Totos. What could be better? She had the greatest best friend and now she had two. As she approached the river she called her two best friends to a halt. They sniffed the ground and each other and then played in the grass together nipping and chasing each other. Donna watched and smiled until a familiar voice was singing/speaking like a Harp being played. It was a familiar voice. Donna scanned along the bank and it did not take long to See her wonderfully , colorful floating friend named Retreat, who asked, "why are you back Donna? We thought you understood and found the answers you were seeking." Donna felt somewhat ashamed of herself, but said,"yes, I did, something else has come up that has me confused." Retreat felt it was her time to help, "Donna, you understand your existence and need to know your journey will have challenges. The Universe has duality, the visible and the invisible. You must know that by now, with your understanding of time. The duality of the universe has different realms of reality. You have your own rhythms within that are set. You must be flexible and believe. You are not capable of knowing everything. Why are you trying so hard?" Donna replied, "I'm not certain. I think that someone has intentionally moved me into this state of mind. I should go now, Thank you." Retreat sang out, "bye for now, I like your new friend." And she was gone. Donna smiled , thinking , I'm not drugged now and still see my friends, so that is proof enough for me of what is real in my place in time I can continue other thoughts later, now it is time to plan our trip, so she called the dogs and they headed home. Along the way she continued to think. I am not meant to know everything, so maybe I'll let it go.

At home she logged in to her lap top and began planning the trip. She booked luxury lodge accommodations at the base of the grand canyon that they would get to by hiking down from the south rim. She would tell John and the kids when they arrived home. She did not have any ideas for dinner so she would wait for the family to get home and let them decide. With time to kill she scrolled through work mail and then called Nancy. Donna asked Nancy if the name Tom Snyder was familiar. Nancy said, " No, Donna, what are you doing? You must let John handle this." Donna lied, " I am , I met a new client that said he knew you, that is all."Donna felt bad for lying. Nancy said, "No, he must be mistaken, never heard of him." Donna said, "okay, thanks, everything is going good." She lied again and then said goodbye. She knew what she saw and came up empty again. She was frustrated and confused so she remembered, you can not know everything, not now. Could her mind have been playing cruel tricks on her, the remnants of hallucinations? NO, think of something else she told herself. The only thing she thought of was hungry, too much thinking made her hungry. She had the dogs settled inside. They were worn out from the park and on the bed nuzzled together. She looked in the pantry and fridge. It was settled from what she inventoried, Taco time. She chopped tomatoes, shredded lettuce and cheese and started browning the meat. Chopped fresh cilantro and chili's. She even had sour cream in fridge. Good thing she had the fridge stocked. She took out soft and hard shell tacos from the pantry. When the family got home they would think they were in a kitchen on the Mexico border. The meat was browning with a Sazon seasoning that made the smell of the kitchen mouth watering. The dogs were resting , but also watching. They could smell the stove and watched their master work. The family was thrilled to make their own hard and soft shell tacos as Donna described the planned trip to the Grand Canyon. They were scheduled to leave the day after next. It was a to be an adventure for the family.

The following day Donna packed and prepared for the drive. It would be one day of driving. A stay at a moderate hotel for the night and then a drive to the Canyon. Donna reserved passes for the National park and from there they they would hike down to the bottom and stay at the lodge overnight. Donna packed up the Jeep with the dogs needs and some food and drinks for the family. Her phone began buzzing and chiming It was Nancy. She said, " Donna I am concerned. I looked up that name and it was the address that John met me at. A psychiatrist, what is happening? What are you doing Donna?" Donna felt stunned. She said, "I was trying to figure some things out, I'm sorry I lied to you." Nancy said, " John wanted to talk to me about LSD. That man, I do not know. Are you ok?" Donna said, " yes, I was feeling confused about many things, but no matter what, I have learned so much. We are taking a trip tomorrow so I have to pack and get ready, see you next week." Donna continued to prepare for the trip. It was impossible not to think. Why would John want to meet Nancy there to talk about LSD? It didn't make any sense or add up to any thing. Nancy and Tom both deny knowing each other. John is the common denominator. What does this all mean? Should she ask him about what she was thinking. No, she had to trust him and her friend. She told herself, to not try to understand everything and to live in her particular place in time. It felt impossible to be patient. John came home and parked in the drive while she was going in and out packing some final things. He hugged and kissed her and then said he would go and pack his bag and see if the kids needed help.

CHAPTER 23

Donna was organizing the Jeep, making room for more and leaving room for the dogs. Her phone started buzzing and chiming. She looked at the number, it wasn't a contact, but she thought the number was familiar so she answered. It was the Psychiatrist, Tom. He asked for her, Mrs. Murphy. He said he had the number from when she called him. She felt very uneasy and asked what she could do for him. He asked her to come to his office as soon as possible. She told him, "I'm packing to go away on a trip." He said, " I think you are in danger, you should not go on that trip. Please come in to talk to me." She said she couldn't talk and had to go and hung up. She thought, why did he call? Danger? She told herself to let it go. The trip was Whst she needed.

The following morning Donna, John, jack and Emma packed their bags and dogs in the Jeep and were on the road. They stopped for a late lunch/early dinner after many hours of driving. It was a Rest stop exit type of restaurant. The food was as expected, delicious and unhealthy. Fried chicken and waffles, chicken fried steak and meat loaf dinners were favorites. They ordered food they normally did not, club sandwiches with the best tasting bacon, Reuben sandwiches with equally incredible fries, with giant sized soft drinks and sweet teas. They talked and laughed. Donna and Emma used the ladies room and returned to order dessert. They laughed so hard talking about the bathroom and the greasy food restaurant Donna thought she would pee in her pants. After large dishes of ice cream and home made pie they were back on the road. They took containers of left overs for the dogs and let them run in the field after eating to go to the bathroom. They drove for several more hours and then checked in to a hotel for the night. They ordered a pizza for late night snacking. Donna laughed so hard with Emma and her guys her stomach hurt. She and Emma shared a bed the boys did same. The dogs were together sleeping nuzzled together. After a slice of pizza and a Sprite Donna was laying in the bed next to her daughter Emma. She looked at her guys and the dogs and thought she could never be happier as she drifted off to sleep.

They were up and ready to hit the road by mid morning. They would take their time and arrive at the South Rim town of the Grand Canyon national park and check into another hotel for the night and begin their journey down the canyon the following morning. They were on the road again planning to stop for lunch. When the kids were sleeping in the rest seat, John reached over and touched Donna and asked, " are you okay ?, have you left your worries behind?" She said, " yes, I feel so much better, I needed to get away." In the back of her mind she had the words still lingering, 'don't go, you are in danger', but she had to dismiss them. She focused on the road and driving. They stopped for lunch at a restaurant that they saw on a highway exit sign. It said country/family style eating. It was another excellent place to eat, rest and let the dogs out to run, plenty of grass next to the parking area. It had an interesting gift shop for souvenirs, clothes and other collection items. Donna purchased shirts for them with the name of the restaurant and the town name. That evening after a long drive they checked into a hotel next to the park. They were tired so decided to eat early the next morning at a breakfast restaurant they was next to the hotel and get fueled up for the hike.

CHAPTER 24

In the morning they filled up on hot cakes, eggs, hash brown potatoes, ham and bacon with juice and coffee at the breakfast restaurant and were off. They checked into the park and parked the Jeep in the over night designated area. They were of to the trail head thst descended the canyon, but first stopped at a look out point for the breathtaking view of the Canyon. Donna looked at the color and layers of the vast canyon and could only think of time. The one and only constant. The depth, width, colors, layer and magnificence of the canyon. She thought of the time that made the striations of colors, the depth and layers. It was the product of thousands of years. She was in the same place in time of this greatness and in the only place in time and it's dimensions that she wanted to be. They found the trail and were ready to begin the 2-3 hour hike to the base of the csnyon. The trail was beside the wall of the canyon. It was approximately 3 meters wide from the wall to the edge of the trail with drops that were to the bottom. Donna was the first to set the pace for her family. She walked straight to the outer edge of the path. The word 'Danger' was in the back of her mind. She looked at the vastness and drop from the edge. Her feelings and thoughts of her place in time were far overwhelming any thoughts or doubts she may have had.Ben was by her side fearlessly trotting along near the edge. Her thoughts of time, the mysteries of faith and life were replaced by the mystery of Love. She was in her state of existence in time. She felt the mystery of love and life flowing through her as she looked over her shoulder and her family was around her as she walked on the precipice. Emma hurried up to hold her hand and lead the way with her mom. They had backpacks with a change of clothes for the next day, liquids and snacks. At look out points along the trail they stopped to hydrate and rest. The hike to the canyon floor was three hours. The views were far more Devine then a portrait or painting for the eyes. At the base they checked into the lodge. The sleeping quarters were clean and comfortable. There were two dining choices, both with menus that pleased them. It was a long hike down. They all bathed and made themselves presentable to eat in the main dining room that was filled with ambiance.. The dogs were fatigued from the day and trip so we're happy to stay behind and sleep in the bed in the kids room. it was a fine meal, that was well deserved following a long day of trekking down the canyon. Donna went out for a walk along the Colorado river that traversed the canyon floor, adjacent to the lodge. John walked beside her as she gazed at the walls of the canyon. She was not certain of what she preparing to say. Her words were unfiltered, "why John?, why did you do it?" She was the Raptor, the Eagle in a zero sum hunting game. He stopped in his tracks. He turned her by placing his hands on her shoulders and looked her in the eyes. "Donna, my love, my wife, I Hsve been trying to help you." She shook him free and continued, "by drugging me?" Emma's voice was calling, "mom, momma."Emma had approached and was interrupting. Donna said, "not now Emma, wait!!" John was standing before Donna and said, "Donna, honey, you should rest." Donna was doing her best to stay calm. She said, "John, I saw you. I saw you with Nancy and Tom. She could not control her thoughts as Emma called out to her, Momma?!"Johns jaw had dropped as he stood in disbelief. He began to speak , but Emma stepped between her mom and dad. Donna said , "please, it can wait Emma."

Emma said she wanted to tell her something, but didn't want her to be mad. Donna had lost control. John tried move. He took one step to walk away with Emma. Donna now grabbed his shoulders and turned him to face her. Donna continued, "Did you want me sent away? To a sanatarium? Did you and Nancy plan this for me? Does she want my job?" John had tears in his eyes as he said, "I met Nancy to get an understanding of Lysergic acid and I interviewed Dr. Snyder as a suspect.

Emma could not contain herself any longer. She held out a plastic, ziplock bag to show her mom and said, "momma, please don't be mad or hate me." Donna and John were in stunned confusion. Donna took the bag and John asked, "Emma, what is this?" Emma said, "my friend, you know, Jackie. Her older sister, Val, told her that at parties they put one of these squares in their drink and they get happy."Donna and John looked at the bag closely. Little cotton squares with the print of a flower on each. Emma continued almost breathless , " well, I told Jackie you were sad so she gave me some she took from her sister and I put one in your coffee one morning to make you happy, but now your mad. I'm sorry momma, I was trying to make you happy. I know it was wrong and I was stupid." Donna had strange, powerful feelings about the constant of time at this moment. She felt trapped and suffocated in a box of time. She wanted to look at John and say LSD, but her maternal Raptor instinct was too strong. She grabbed Emma and said, "please tell me you never put this in your drinks."Donna grabbed Emma and sobbed in her hair. Emma said, "momma, you are sad now, not mad at me?" John took the bag and said he had to secure it for evidence. He asked Emma in confirmation "you never drank this did you?" She said, "no daddy, I'm sorry, please don't be mad." He hugged her and Donna and said, " no peanut, never. " Donna looked at John and was beginning to speak, to say she was sorry. John held on to her and Emma with one arm and raised his other arm with his palm out signaling for her to stop. Jack's deep voice called out as the dogs ran towards them, "there is fire pit over here, I got stuff for s'mores from the gift shop. Let's make dessert out here!" Emma ran over to jack excited and eager to to have a fire pit party. Donna took John's hand and asked , "are you upset with me?" He said, "not upset any longer, a little disappointed that you lost faith in me, but I understand." She thought 'I can never lose faith in what I believe again' and said, "I'm truly sorry, I never will again, I love you, let's go." The fire pit was roaring thanks to a member of the staff at the lodge. The staff also provided long skewers for roasting marshmallows and trays for the graham crackers and chocolate. It was a perfect picturesque s'mores gathering by the fire with the canyon glowing in the background. Ben sat with his eyes glowing from the fiery flames by Donna's side and the puppy next to Emma with likewise eyes. Donna, John, jack and Emma roasted marshmallows in the flickering flames and then sandwiched them on graham crackers with a slice of Hershey's chocolate melting under the hot marshmallows. It was the perfect dessert following a delicious dinner. The fire glowed casting shadows on the canyon wall. It was a quiet evening as the temperature dropped. The fire created a centrifuge of warmth that was an invisible barrier shielding them from the cool night air. The staff had put a side table out with folded and stacked south west print cotton blankets, similar to the one Donna always had in her Jeep. Emma moved her chair closer to her Mom and asked, "can we stay here forever? " Emma was only fourteen. Donna wanted to explain everything, but did not want to confuse her daughter. She thought deeply and considered. Donna thought it best to explain. Emma broke the moment of silence, "mom, go ahead, tell me what you are thinking, I know that you know. I can see it in your eyes." Donna decided to explain existence and time in a slightly different way. She said, "ok Emma, think of it this way. You have good dreams and bad ones, nightmares. There is day time and night time. You are happy now, you were sad earlier. There is good and bad or you could say good and evil. You can see the moon and stars now. In the morning you will see the sun. A baby will be born at the same moment in time that an old person dies. When you are near the sea the tide brings the sea close to shore and then later the tide pulls the water back out. Life is existence and it is forever changing, yet always here. The only constant is time. Old man time or Father Time stops for nothing and no one. We exist in time. We are part of the constant. Let me show you." Donna took two marshmallows. She browned one and blackened the other. She asked Emma to take a bite of each. Then continued, "one is sweet to the taste, the other is bitter. You know the good and the bad. You walk securely and confident, not stumble in your existence. You are proof. You do not shudder in fear of a storm that strikes, you know it will pass. As we sit in this moment we know it will pass. We exist in time. We will always be here just as this canyon has been. Look in your mind and believe. You can talk to God and loved ones that are no longer here and you know they are with you. The day, the night, the good, the bad, it is all occurring in time. We do not have control of it. We can not escape or control the Universe created by God. Accept and have faith in what you know to be the proof as I have explained We are here now. We will always have this place in time. Time will continue forever into eternity. Just as time is consistent and owns its nature, we will always be here and own our existence in time. " Donna looked to Emma, hoping she understood. Emma was sleeping in John's arms like a baby. Jack had fallen asleep in his Adirondack style chair. The fire was smoldering down to hot coals with a couple of logs still flickering from the coals below. There was the side table with clean southwest cotton blankets, similar to hers in the Jeep. Donna covered her family with the blankets and took the trays and skewers in to the lodge and found the kitchen for the dining room where they ate. She placed the trays and skewers on a stainless steel sink table and headed back to the fire pit outside to gather up her family and get them to beds. As Donna approached the fire pit outside she could hear Emma talking, " are you happy Daddy? Are you sure I said the right thing?" John replied, " yes peanut, you did good and I love you." Donna felt odd and thought, 'what does that mean?' Then told herself to stop and clapped her hands twice, then said, "time for bed people, get up, let's go!" It was a long, fun day. They tucked into bed and were fast asleep knowing in the morning they were to hike back up the canyon. Ben and Shelby had a long day and sat by the fire with them late. They were equally or more tired and slept soundly by the bed of Donna and John.

CHAPTER 25

The following morning the sunlight found its way into the canyon as the family packed and prepared to hike back up. Donna walked outside of the lodge and stretched with arms up to the sun after a restful night of sleep. She had washed off the fire pit smoke and felt refreshed. A Raptor was soaring across the blue sky and her mind returned to the words of the night before, "daddy, are you happy, did I say the right thing?" She heard the words in her mind and looked at the bird soaring, the zero sum existence of the Raptor and her belief that existence is not zero sum. She thought, ' be fearless in your belief'. I must believe in my little girl if she is to believe in me. Donna walked back inside. They sat in the dining room , ordered egg omelets, hot cakes, hash brown potatoes and bacon with pitchers of orange juice to energize for the days long hike ahead. They had food and treats for the dogs. They ate heartily knowing that hiking up was more challenging then descending. They went back to the rooms one last time before checking out at the lobby of the lodge to get their packs and the dogs. Donna was in the bathroom one last time when she stopped to check herself in the mirror. She saw no reflection in the mirror and felt strangely dizzy. She touched the mirror glass and looked, but saw nothing. She thought it is time to go. It struck her light an electric shock again, TIME. She thought to herself, ' have I gone too far, explored too much. Maybe there are things I should not know. Have I told Emma too much?' She remembered what her little floating fairy friends had told her, ' you can not know everything now'. She walked out and they all headed for the trail. As they approached the trail head, a narrow path that ascended out of the canyon Donna led the way. Moments before she began Ben ran up beside her, grabbed her pant leg in his mouth and pulled her. She took his leash out of her back pack and attached it to his collar. Ben gripped the leash in his jaws and pulled her back. He wanted her to go with him. His primordial instinct knew it was time for her to go. His limited cognitive thought knew Love and he could not let her go as a human can not accept the loss of a loved one The puppy , Shelby, ran off up the path. Donna dropped the leash and followed Shelby up the path to her destiny.

The earth began to rumble and move as the wall of the canyon vibrated. Ben barked and cried out loudly. Ben wasbegging Donna to come with him. It was too late. . She could not know. Ben was calling as Donna ran after Shelby up the trail. Large chunks of rock and swells of gravel fell from above. It was suddenly as if the canyon wall had fallen off following tens of thousands of years forming through time with the shifting of the earth's surface and plates in the ice, snow and sun. Now it was a great pile of rock and clay. Donna was buried inside of it.

She heard someone calling her name. 'Mrs. Murphy? Mrs. Murphy!' She looked up and saw Dr. Belmont. He said, " Ben is gone now, would like to take him or would you like us to dispose of him?" She got up and ran out of the waiting area of the Veterinarian's office and looked around. She saw Emma standing next to a pile of rock and rubble crying. Donna went to her and said. " Emma, Shelby I'm here, look Emma I'm here.. , do you understand, I will be here with you forever." All of existence was now clear for Donna. She saw everything. Emma thought , ' yes momma, I understand, I believe in you and everything you told me. We Will be here forever. '. As she thought 'why is she calling to Shelby. Emma looked down as she felt Ben stretching up to her with his front paws on her leg. Ben was staring at the pile of rock and clay and reaching for Emma. Emma said, "yes Ben, I see you too." She picked him up and hugged him with his head in her neck. "Ben, momma is here with us." She let him down and walked to the Colorado river nearby with him. Emma sat on the bank of the river with Ben by her side. He was searching the bank of the river with his eyes waiting for something. Emma looked over at him. His head was no longer searching the bank. It was hung and she thought he was weeping. Ben hung hung his head not capable of knowing time and existence. He would Love Donna forever. Emma placed her arm around him and pulled him close, then said, " if Momma was here she wouldn't want to see you like this." Emma's eyes welled, a tear fell from her eye. Ben reached his head up and licked the tear from her cheek. Emma placed her head on his head and said, "Momma is here." Donna looked up at the sun as a bird glided across the sky and cast a shadow. She thought, ' most are reluctant to leave their present state of existence, in fear of the unknown. She thought of a parable from scripture that father O'Donnell had once quoted and used as a metaphor, explaining life and heaven to the congregation, 'a family of sea lions lived in the desert. They had a good life. When they inevitably passed on from their present life they found themselves living in the ocean water. They loved life, knowing no other. They had only known the desert , but found that they loved living in and belonged in the sea. 'Yay, though Donna walked through the valley of the shadow of death', she feared not. (Psalm 23:4) she was walking through time and existence...........................

Time moved on
The Wonder.

The-quest and journey was complete. Donna now understood. She was unable to know everything until now. All oF TIME was now in one state. The past, present and future were ONE in TIME.

Alex, Shelby, Mom, Dad, uncle Elison, her fairy friends, John, jack, Emma, Ben and all she had ever known and loved were existing in the Universe in unison. The dimensions were all clearly in unison. There was no need, want or use for scientific evidence. The feelings and emotions she felt were more gratifying and pleasing than that of any equation or problem she had ever solved. She felt as she thought the sea lions would, discovering their natural existence in the ocean. It was a long, trying journey traveling through her life. It was all well worth it now. John and jack had joined Emma and Ben at the riverbank. They were encircled by the bright, glowing yellow light. There were no equations, no theories, no data. All of the mysteries, life, love, faith, existence were solved. It simply took TIME. There was nothing to fear nor doubt